Becoming His

USA TODAY BESTSELLING AUTHOR

K.I. LYNN

Becoming His

Copyright © K.I. Lynn

Cover design by Opium House Creatives

Editor
Evident Ink
Marti Lynch
Missy Borucki

Publication Date: April 17, 2019
Genre: FICTION/Romance/Contemporary
ISBN-13: 978-1948284097

BLACKOUT: A Romance Anthology

Close Encounter by Stephanie St. Klaire
"The day started with a quick screw, a couple of quirky two-bit cons and ended
with a diabolical serial killer. What do you do when the lights go out? Run."

The Do-Over by Christi Barth
"The best way to move on after being dumped? A hot fling. An even better way?
Revenge sex and the chance to turn the tables on the guy who dumped you..."

Night & Day by Bethany Lopez
"One explosive weekend together nearly ruined them. But, there's no way Simone
and Micah can ignore their chemistry when they're alone in the dark."

Night Games by T.K. Leigh
"Note to self: Never agree to play an innocent dice game during a blackout in
Vegas. I should have known it wouldn't remain innocent, not in the city of sin."

Absolutely Mine by Terri E. Laine
"I made a promise to stay away from my best friend's little sister. But it's Vegas
and that's one promise I'm probably going to break."

Just Us by J.H. Croix
"Ellie asks me to promise her one thing. We can't tell her brother about us. Small
problem though. One night will never be enough."

Blind Faith by Lauren Runow
"I never expected to be locked out of my room basically naked in a total blackout.
Thinking that would be the biggest shock of my night was my first mistake."

Dirty Thoughts by C.A. Harms
"He was the crush I never thought I'd see again. Yet here we were in Vegas,
during a total blackout. I figure why not explore all the possibilities, or more like
let him explore me?"

Going Down by Lisa Shelby
"She's the only person I've ever loved and I'm the last person she wants to see.
She'd hoped to avoid me as much as possible in Vegas, but when we get stuck
alone in an elevator, not even she can deny that our chemistry still runs hot."

Hard Luck by K.A. Ware

"Ellis James is my kryptonite, the only person who could drag me back to Vegas after I promised myself I was done with that life. I'd bleed for her, I'd die for her, but can I save her?"

Becoming His by K.I. Lynn
When I slammed into Hollywood heartthrob Reid Gallagher, I never imagined it would turn into a first date I'd never forget. After all, what happens in Vegas, stays in Vegas...right?

Honeymoon Hideaway by Cary Hart
What's worse than being locked in a room with a vibrating bed and your sworn enemy? Waking up next to him... naked! Did I mention he's also my boss? Oops.

Free Bird by Leddy Harper
"She's a showgirl who wants out of Vegas. He's a rugby player who wants a bit of company. Can they both get what they want?"

To learn more about our contributors, and their stories:
www.privatepartybookclub.com/blackout

CHAPTER ONE

January 12th

"Welcome to Las Vegas. Local time is 9:27. Current temperature is forty-three degrees and sunny. We thank you for flying with us and look forward to seeing you all again. From the entire flight crew, we hope you have a fabulous stay," the captain said over the intercom.

"Finally," Sarah sighed loudly in the seat next to me.

"That was the longest flight ever." My muscles were thankful for the first stretch in hours.

"It just felt like that."

We pulled our bags down from the overhead and waited to exit the plane. As soon as we were off, the sweet sounds and bright, flashing lights of the airport slot machines called to us. I had to grab Sarah's hand as she angled for a bank of them.

"But..."

"Just think of all the machines waiting for us at the hotel."

With a small pout, she conceded and we continued on our path to baggage claim. The walk was endless, our spot at the end of what seemed like a mile's worth of carousels. We wrangled four suitcases from the moving platform, and only one of them was mine. The others were filled with various wedding paraphernalia. After the luggage debacle, we headed to the curbside pickup to hail a taxi.

"Why didn't we order a car?" Sarah asked as we looked at the line—at least fifty people were ahead of us.

I narrowed my eyes on her as we sat at the end. "That's what I asked you. More than once."

Thankfully there seemed to be a pretty steady flow. After a fifteen-minute wait, the driver of a minivan loaded our bags into the back.

"Let me get that for you," he said with a smile as he held the door open for me.

"Thank you." I slid in and found Sarah staring at me. "What?"

"He's flirting with you."

"He's just being nice."

The cabbie slid in and turned to us, his eyes locked on me. "Where to, ladies?"

Sarah's elbow swung out and tapped me. "The Tyrrhenian, please."

He turned back around, but I caught his eyes in the rearview mirror. They were dark, but soft, very friendly, and he wasn't bad on the eyes at all.

"Can you take us down the strip?" Sarah asked.

"You sure? That costs more."

She nodded. "She's never been here before."

My eyes were wide as I stared at the massive complexes of the mammoth hotels, each different and unique. The driver was acting like a tour guide, giving us the history and names of each one.

"Wow," I said as I stared in amazement.

"Right? Told you it was something."

About halfway through our trip, I noticed the driver turn off the meter.

We pulled up to a massive white marble and aqua glass drop-off to the hotel. There were crystals hanging everywhere, making everything sparkle and the lights bounce all over as they glinted off the faceted edges, sleek and modern with a sea-like feel.

"How long are you in town for?" he asked as he unloaded the bags, his eyes on me. It was almost like Sarah wasn't even there.

"For the week."

"Maybe I'll run into you again. I'm Sam." He held out his hand, and I slipped mine in.

"Harper."

"Well, Harper, if I don't get to see you again, have a great week."

"Thanks, Sam," I said as I bit down on my lip.

Behind Sam, I could see Sarah making gestures and mouthing something, finally landing on the pound sign.

With another warm smile, Sam got back in the car and I stepped over to Sarah and the heap of luggage.

"Why didn't you give him your number?" Sarah asked when I turned to her.

"I don't know him."

"Duh. You don't know anybody until you get to know them, and that was the perfect opportunity to have some fun with a good-looking guy this week."

"Let me work up to it, okay?"

Her lips formed a thin line. "Fine, but promise me you will not shoot down every guy."

"I'll try."

The Tyrrhenian was the newest hotel on the strip, taking the place of one of Vegas's older, failed establishments. It was still in its soft opening, gearing up for a hard opening on Saturday.

The hotel wasn't as nuance themed as many of the other on the strip. It had a modern ocean theme. Clean, crisp colors, with shades of blue and aqua that danced across the marble floors.

The lobby was packed with people checking out, but thankfully there was a separate line for check-ins. Sarah had requested early check-in, and we didn't have to wait for a room, which was great because jet lag had taken over.

"Are you sure you're up to this?" Sarah asked as I threw my backpack onto the bed.

"I'm fine," I replied, but she gave me that look, the one your best friend gave when she knew your bullshit and she caught you in it.

"Really?" she stressed.

"Really, seriously."

"There are times you're going to be on your own," she reminded me.

"I know." I wasn't Sarah's maid of honor—that roll was reserved for her sister Anna—I was her best friend and only other bridesmaid. There were a lot of final things she and her fiancé had to do before the big day.

Vegas was their favorite vacation spot, and they decided on a small destination wedding. There were only about fifty people, closest friends and family, traveling out and attending.

She'd convinced me to leave winter in Ohio for Las Vegas on Sunday, four days earlier than my original plan. After all, I had the vacation time, thanks to it rolling over from the previous year.

Actually, it was thanks to my ex-boyfriend Jeremy breaking up with me a month before we were supposed to go to the Bahamas—a trip I didn't go on alone.

Sarah let out a sigh. "I wanted you to come out to Vegas with me to renew yourself, but I didn't think about how much there was to do to get ready for the wedding after I pick Rob up on Tuesday."

"I'm not dead," I said as I toed off my shoes.

"No. But your social life is."

"We still have time for some fun. That gives us all of today and tomorrow and most of Tuesday to drink and gamble."

"And see a show."

I groaned. Sarah was obsessed with the shows. She and Rob spent an entire week just going to as many as they could cram in.

"Remind me how you managed to land this hotel," I said as I flopped down on one of the beds, a contented moan leaving me as I sank into its softness.

"Rob's uncle is the hotel manager."

"It's going to be the first wedding here, isn't it?"

She nodded and lay back on the other bed. "What do you want to do first?"

"Nap."

"Seriously?"

"Seriously," I stressed as I pulled the edge of the duvet to cover myself. "We left at nine and got here at nine. We take an hour nap, freshen up, and explore."

"Hmm, I might be down with this plan," she said and immediately began to choke hold one of the pillows.

"That way we'll be on local time faster," I pointed out.

"I'm not finding many holes."

"It's because there are none. Sleep, freshen up, food and booze—in that order."

"Gambling?"

I popped my head out from underneath the cover. "That goes with the booze number two."

"Booze number two?"

"Booze number one is with food."

"Ahh, you want to get shit-faced." The last word triggered a yawn before she settled back into her wrestling position. I often wondered how she slept with Rob. Did she do the same maneuver with him?

"They've got yards of margaritas around here somewhere, right?"

She fanned her hand in front of her. "Pretty sure somewhere."

"I want to try every flavor."

"We need a DBG."

"What?"

"Designated bodyguard. Someone to make sure we don't get ourselves killed or kidnapped while we're a hundred proof and throwing up on the streets."

My eyes were heavy, the drowsiness taking over, body weighted. "We've been watching too much *Abducted at First Sight*. And, dude, I want to get wasted, not poisoned. You go that far and tomorrow is over, and there are still things I want to do before I lose you to the man."

"Mm hmm," Sarah responded.

That was the last I heard before sleep took me.

I startled awake at a blaring noise, my heart nearly jumping out of my chest. "Shit!"

"Mmm, hey, babe," Sarah said into her phone. "Yeah, sorry. We got in and immediately crashed for a little while."

I grabbed my phone, noticing it was at forty percent, and also the time, but the time didn't register until I was pulling my cord from my purse.

"Shit."

"What?" Sarah asked, pausing her conversation.

I looked over to her. "We slept for almost two hours."

"Shit, indeed."

A yawn and a deep stretch was the first step to waking up. While the nap did help, I was in need of an espresso or energy drink to get my brain going again.

It was the first time I got a good look at the room. The color scheme from the lobby continued into the rooms. A textured wallpaper of aqua and gold adorned one wall, there was a white dresser that had a few drawers and a small fridge against the opposite wall, a desk on one side with a white desk chair, and two aqua-colored sofa chairs near the window with a gold painted table between them. The lamps had a mercury glass-like look with off-white shades that matched the carpet, which was textured with aqua waves.

Moving to the window, I opened the blackout curtains all the way, then the privacy shade. I stared out in awe at the view of the few hotels in sight. They were all so huge that only the ones directly in front of the hotel could be seen.

After digging out my toiletry bag, I headed into the bathroom. It was huge, taking up more room than I anticipated with a large walk-in shower and marble sink. A large lighted mirror sat over the counter, and I scared myself with the reflection of my raccoon eyes. The only nice thing was how it made my green eyes pop.

My brunette hair was also sticking everywhere and in need of some taming. All in all, I needed a lot of help before I was presentable.

"Rob says hi," Sarah said as she entered the bathroom.

"What did he think of the plan?" I asked.

"He said be careful and it better result in you getting laid."

"Ha! He would say that." I wasn't exactly opposed to the idea of having fun with someone this week, but I wasn't a one-night-stand kind of person. I'd never had one before.

Then again, there was a first time for everything.

CHAPTER TWO

After freshening up, which included redoing my hair and makeup and sifting through all the clothes I brought with me, we made our way down to the lobby. The jeans, Mary Jane wedges, and a front-tie V-neck with embroidered flowers on the shoulders was the most I'd dressed up in months, and it wasn't much.

I wore yoga pants and a T-shirt to work, and I hadn't been in the mood to go out since the breakup. I didn't even go out for New Year's Eve, opting instead for my pajamas and watching movies with my niece.

We'd barely stepped out of the elevator when Sarah glanced at her phone and cursed.

"Shit, do you have your power bank on you?" she asked before we'd gotten too far from the elevator bay.

I stopped in my tracks. "It's in the room. Want me to grab it?"

She twirled her finger in the air. "Pretty please. I'll be over at the Seaside bar getting us some margaritas."

"K." I turned and sprinted back to the elevator bay.

A door closed right when I got there, but I spotted a door at the end still open.

"Wait!" I sprinted over and slipped through the gap as the doors closed. "Oh!" I cried as I slammed into a chest. Hands wrapped around my waist, sending a shock through me as they steadied me.

"Whoa!"

"Oh, my God, I'm so sorry," I said as I tried to pull back, my gaze flashing to the man I pretty much tackled. All the blood rushed to my cheeks as I stared at piercing grey eyes that held a glint of amusement.

He was gorgeous. Perfectly tousled brown hair, strong features, and a solid physique that was evident from the fabric of his dress shirt practically stretching from the muscles underneath. He towered over my 5'3" frame, which was heightened another three inches due to my shoes, easily passing six foot. His shoulders were broad, a five o'clock shadow accentuated his strong jaw, and did I mention the muscles?

"A beautiful woman throwing herself at me will never get old," he said in a deep, smooth voice.

"I-I...what—" I was frazzled, completely speechless and an utter clusterfuck. I gasped, realizing I was still pressed against him, then stepped away in total and complete embarrassment.

The elevator was already whizzing up the shaft, and I turned toward the panel. A surge of panic ran through me as I stared at it, trying to read the numbers, but was confused when the numbers started at fifty.

"What? Where are the other numbers?"

"Are you in a suite?" Mr. Gorgeous asked.

"No."

Suddenly the elevator slowed and shook, the lights flickering. Instinctively I reached out and grabbed onto the stranger next to me as the car shuddered to a stop. My eyes widened, and I dug my nails into his forearm as panic settled in. My stomach turned, and it felt like my body was vibrating.

"Hey, it's okay," he said, trying to catch my eyes. "Look at me."

My gaze found his as my jaw locked down. I suffered from a little bit of claustrophobia, but I was good with elevator rides as long as they kept going.

"I'm guessing you just jumped into any elevator," he said, pulling my attention away from whatever was happening.

I nodded. "I wasn't thinking. I just saw an open door."

"It's okay. I won't snitch on you," he said with a smirk.

His eyes were so beautiful, clear, and I was swept up in them. It was the distraction I needed. He was so warm and strong, his presence filling the small space and wrapping around me.

The elevator gave another shake before continuing its climb, and I let out a sigh of relief.

"What was that?" I asked.

"New hotel. Just a hiccup," he assured me.

I nodded, trying to believe that he was right, but my imagination was attempting to override that. "So, this is the expensive rooms elevator?"

"Yeah."

I blew out a breath and leaned against the wall. "Well, this is going to make my quick run to my room a bit longer." He chuckled at that. Something about his expression I'd seen before, but I couldn't place it. "You look familiar, but in an out-of-place kinda way."

"What does that mean?" he asked, but that smirk stayed. He knew what I was talking about.

"Like, I know who you are, but you're not in the setting I know you from. Make sense?"

He nodded. "I can see that."

"But I'm the only one feeling it."

He grinned at me. "Yup."

"You're not going to help me out, are you?"

"Nope. This is just too much fun." The elevator slowed, and he turned to me. "Have you ever seen a penthouse suite?"

"No."

The car came to a stop. "Want to?" The door slid open and he held out his arm, gesturing me to step forward.

I looked at him and stepped through. "You're not a serial killer luring me to your room so you can chop me up, are you?"

"That's pretty descriptive," he said with a chuckle, pulling his phone from his back pocket.

"I watch way too much of the Investigation Discovery channel."

"Not a serial killer, but I have played one." He tapped his screen, and the distinctive click of the lock echoed around the tile floor.

Played one?

His familiarity crashed into me. "Oh my God. You're Reid Gallagher."

There was a sparkle in his eye as he turned the handle. "You were about to give me a complex."

I could do nothing but stare at him in shock. I'd run into Reid Gallagher without even trying. His hands had been on me.

The door swung open, and music and the sounds of people talking flowed out of the opening.

"Come on in."

I blinked at him, at his outstretched hand, then to the movement inside. "Really?"

"Why not?" His brows knit together in confusion.

"Because I'm a weird girl who tackled you in an elevator?" And I would throw myself at him again if given half the chance, even before I knew his celebrity status.

"All the more reason." There was a wolfish grin playing on his lips.

"So your security knows what I look like to make sure I'm nowhere near you?"

That made him laugh out loud, his head thrown back. His reaction got the attention of a guy walking by and he headed toward us, his brow cocked as he stared at me.

"Reid, dude, what's going on?" the guy asked as he eyed me.

"This is my new friend..." he trailed off and looked to me for help.

"Oh. Harper. My name's Harper," I said like an idiot. Then again, I was struck a bit stupid by my realization of who I was standing next to.

"Harper, meet Kalvin."

"You're making friends?" Kalvin asked, eyeing Reid. "I thought you were just riding down with Tre."

"We just bumped into each other," Reid said, giving me a wink.

Bump was a bit of an understatement, but it was nice that he didn't paint me as a fanatic who accosted him.

He nodded. "Cool. Come on in, girly. Let's take a look at our new friend."

"*Our*?" I asked, glancing at Reid.

"Any friend of Reid's is a friend of his crew."

I followed Reid in, and I glanced around in awe at the space. The memory of only seeing three doors flashed in my mind.

Holy shit, it was huge. Easily ten-foot ceilings, wide-open living room, full kitchen, even its own bar that looked fully stocked. The floor-to-ceiling windows let in a ton of light from the afternoon sun.

Kalvin gave some introductions. "That there is Lou, and in the blue is Anthony. That fine thing over there is Kiki." He pointed to a stylish brunette who was talking to the only other woman in the room besides me.

"Kimber," Reid corrected.

"It's Kiki, get over it."

"Mom named her Kimber."

"Oh, you want to get into what your mom named you two, do you?"

Reid's eyes widened, and he threw his hands up. "I yield, but don't expect me to call her that."

"Whatever." Kalvin waved him off. "So, before *Reid* interrupted me, that's my girl *Kiki*. As you may have figured out, she's Reid's baby sister."

Kalvin went over a few more names of the near dozen other people, but the only one I remembered besides his was Kiki.

"I'm hearing my name an awful lot over here," Kiki said as she slipped her arm around Kalvin's waist.

"Hey, baby." He leaned down and kissed her lips.

By the non-reaction from her brother, I gathered they'd been together for a long time.

"I was just showing Reid's new friend the crew."

She blinked at me, then looked to Reid. "New friend? You made a friend? You left ten minutes ago."

Reid shrugged and pointed to himself. "Chick magnet. I drew her to me like she was made of metal. Couldn't resist me."

"That's how it went down, huh?" I asked with a roll of my eyes and a knock of my elbow.

"Exactly."

Kiki pursed her lips, not a hint of the amusement we shared in her expression. "So, no offense," she sneered and held up her hand to me, which I found more offensive than her words, "you picked up some random chick from the lobby and decided you were friends on the ride up?"

"Why is this an issue?" Reid asked, tone changing, friction tensing the air around us.

"Because you don't make friends that fast."

Reid shrugged and smiled at her, but it was forced. "There's a first time for everything."

Kiki looked between us. "Be careful with him," she warned before stomping away. Kalvin gave a shrug and went after her.

It confused me, especially since I'd known him a whopping fifteen minutes, if that long, but I supposed due to the nature of his stardom, it was to be expected.

"Come on, sit with me," Reid said, his hand sliding into mine.

I drew in a sharp breath at his touch, an electric bite sinking into my skin and spreading through me from the spot. Reid's gaze shot down to our hands. Had the spark been that strong in the elevator?

His grip tightened as he led us across the large room, away from the crowd.

The large open space had two sitting areas separated by a fireplace that was a small barrier between the two. The fireplace could be seen from both sides, creating a window into the other space. Definitely large enough to see Kiki eyeing me. There was a couch with two cushions and we each took one, our hands reluctantly separating.

The whole situation was surreal. What in the world was I doing? I couldn't understand why he had me stay, but I was happy.

Seconds ticked by as we looked at each other, then looked away, both seeming to search for something to break the awkwardness that surrounded us since he took my hand.

"What brings you to Vegas?" I asked, then suddenly began backpedaling, because he was Reid Gallagher and he could go wherever the hell he wanted and he didn't owe me any explanation. Basically, I freaked out, suddenly very self-conscious about the whole situation. "Not that something needs to bring you. You can go anytime you want."

He chuckled at my awkwardness. "I'm filming a new movie here."

"In this hotel?"

He nodded. "Yeah. I can't tell you the title, or really much about it, but I can tell you it's got a lot of action."

"Is that why all the extra muscles?"

"You noticed," he said as he flexed.

"Yeah, well, they're kinda out there and huge, and I don't remember you looking quite so buff in *Tremble*, and there were a lot of shirtless scenes. So, yeah, I noticed."

His head fell back in laughter. "I'm beginning to think maybe you weren't so innocent in your accosting."

"Total innocence."

"Maybe. So, what's your story?" he asked. "Where are you from? Is throwing yourself at unsuspecting men a hobby?"

I slapped my hands over my face, hiding my eyes. "Don't say it like that. Oh my God."

"You did throw yourself at me."

"That was an accident. I threw myself through the opening. Not my fault you were in the way."

He leaned back, his brow cocked. "In the way? Oh, wow."

"Like a brick wall," I said with a nod, then slapped my hands together. "Stopped me dead in my tracks."

"It was my animal magnetism. You can admit it, it's all right."

I shook my head, unable to knock the smile from my face. Funny and charming and hot and—he had one too many of my favorite characteristics in a man.

"To finish answering your questions, I'm from Ohio. Cincinnati area."

He angled himself toward me. "Wait, you're from Cincinnati?"

"Suburbs. Mason, to be exact. Why?"

He smiled. "I'm from Loveland."

My mouth popped open. "You're kidding me."

He shook his head. "We moved out here when I was fifteen, but before that, I was a Tiger."

"And my sworn enemy."

"You Comets always acting like the world is going to end."

"Oooh!" I leaned back, eyes wide.

A huge grin spread on his face. "Yeah, you see what I just did there."

"Technically, that's an asteroid," I said, bursting his bubble.

His expression fell, and he gave me a teasing glare. "Don't get all technical. Just bask in my wordplay."

I laughed and shook my head. "Wow. Small world."

"Yeah."

Without warning, I let out a loud yawn, unable to stop it.

"Am I boring you?" he asked.

I shook my head, trying to indicate adamantly that it was in no way him. "No, sorry. The time difference is catching up to me and I am in desperate need of some caffeine."

"Any preference on the caffeine?"

"As long as it's not horrible, I suppose not. Why?"

He signaled over to Kiki. "Hey, Kimber, are there still some *Rockstar* cans over there?"

She moved over to the kitchen and pulled open the fridge. "Yeah, you've got a bunch."

"Be a lamb."

She shook her head. "Shithead," she cursed as she grabbed a can and brought it over, handing it to Reid.

"Thanks," he said before passing it over to me.

"Thank you," I said to Kiki. She stared at me for a moment before her lips curled up into a smile.

"Oh, she likes you," Reid said with a smirk, earning a glare from Kiki before she walked back over to Kalvin. He leaned in once she was gone. "She's a tough one, so it's a big deal to get a smile."

I popped open the can and greedily gulped the liquid down. "Does your crew stay here as well?" I asked, peeking through the glass of the fireplace to see his family and friends talking, some laughing, but still watching us from the corner of their eyes. They were curious, not that I blamed them. I was a nobody. A stranger he found in the hotel's elevator and brought up to hang out.

"No, all me. They just visit," Reid said, pulling my attention back to him. He was shaking his head, an amused smile curling up at the edge of his lips.

Lips that I found myself continuously drawn to.

He had to be a great kisser.

"All this for yourself, then?"

It was a lame question, but it seemed odd to me. He rose a brow, an action that once again showcased his storm-cloud eyes. "I need my alone time just like anyone else."

"But if there are always people here…"

"They're not usually all here, but I'm not shooting today, so we're relaxing. At least for a little while. I have to work out and go over some things for tomorrow."

My heart beat wildly in my chest, and that was when I noticed he'd shifted closer.

No, not just him. Me, too. I was inches from where I'd been, one thigh resting in the crack between the cushions, which tilted me even closer. His hand sat on the small fabric that showed between my thigh and his.

Far enough to be decent, but close enough that if he shifted, his pinky would graze my skin.

I couldn't decide if it had been so long since I'd felt an attraction to anyone that my reaction to him was hitting me hard, or if the pull I felt was just that overpowering.

"Sorry, I'm just fascinated by all this." I shrugged sheepishly, wanting to know everything, halfway hoping he'd invite me to watch him work out.

"What do you do?" he asked, continuing on with our *getting to know you*.

"Nothing as fantastic as this." I waved a hand around. "I'm a physical therapist."

"Really? That's still awesome." His facial expression held a mixture of surprise and... intrigue?

"Maybe she can help you massage out that issue you're having," some guy said with a laugh from the other side of the room, grabbing his junk.

No one else laughed.

Reid tensed beside me, muscles coiled tight as the hand next to my thigh clenched. His gaze narrowed on him. "Out."

The guy held out his arms. "What? Why?"

"Reid said out," Kalvin said as he pointed toward the door.

"This is bullshit." The guy glared around the room, probably hoping someone would take his side, before throwing his can down and stomping out. He made sure to slam the door extra hard on his way out.

My gaze shot from the door to Reid. "What was that all about?"

"A little ribbing and vulgarity."

"Oh. Massage..." The guy was talking about Reid's—oh my God.

My face flamed red hot as mortification settled in.

Wrong moment to be slow on the uptake. Then again, I was still enamored by the man inches from me. He was quite distracting.

"One problem with having a crew is they know pretty much everything about your life. Including the personal shit. Now, back to you. Physical therapy, huh?"

I nodded. "Yeah. I work in sports therapy and rehabilitation."

"Like injured athletes?" he asked.

"Exactly. From kids to pros."

"Pros?" There was something in his tone that I couldn't identify.

"Oh, yeah. I've got this major league pain in my ass. He actually demanded I fly back for his normal therapy days."

His eyes narrowed. "Seriously?"

"He tried to say he'd pay for the flights, and when I refused, he went off with 'What the fuck do I pay you for?' to which I reminded him that he didn't pay me, his insurance company and the ball club did."

"Are you fucking serious?" Reid seemed genuinely outraged on my behalf.

"Yeah, there are some entitled assholes out there. I work *with* you, not *for* you. There's a big difference, and if you treat me shitty, I'll kick you out as my client."

"Good. I wouldn't be shitty. I'd be the model client."

I gave him a quick look up and down. "Uh huh."

"Seriously."

"You know, I was promised a tour of this penthouse suite," I said. It was getting a little weird to have half a dozen people staring in our general direction.

"Did I say tour?"

"Well, you asked me if I'd ever seen a penthouse suite, which indicated an offering for me to see it, and I don't think this area is all there is to see."

"Hmm, you're right. What was I thinking?"

"I've been wondering that for a while, but I wasn't going to say anything."

He stood and held his hand out. "Come on."

I slipped my hand in his and he gave a yank, pulling me to my feet. Besides the two living areas, there was also a full-sized kitchen, exquisite dining room, full bar that looked like it belonged in the lobby, an entry, and a lot of space not even my house could measure up to.

There were two good-sized bedrooms, then back across the space, near where we'd been sitting, was the master.

"Wow, this room is huge," I said as I looked around the bedroom and into the adjoining bathroom. "I think it's bigger than our whole room." The bed was larger than a normal king size. It looked soft and fluffy like a cloud, and I couldn't stop myself from running and throwing myself down on it to test it out.

When I landed, I could hear Reid laugh as I sank into the plush mattress.

"Heaven," I sighed as I relaxed into the bed, a smile playing on my lips.

"That is a heavenly view," Reid said.

I turned to look at him, and when our eyes met, a shiver ran through me. I froze, unable to move, unable to comprehend the charge in the air.

It was then I realized I'd just thrown myself onto the man's bed, ass up. Embarrassment flooded through me, heat filling my cheeks.

"Sorry," I said as I slid off.

He held out his hand and pulled me to my feet, then right into his chest. The muted voices of his crew in the other rooms disappeared entirely as we stood there.

"Nothing to be sorry about." His voice was low, and an electric spark exploded on my skin from each point of our contact.

What was going on?

It almost felt like energy crackling between us with an intensity I'd never experienced before. The air was heavy, and everything seemed to fall away except the man in front of me.

His mouth opened to say something when my phone chimed, breaking the thickness of the tension that rose between us.

"Sorry," I said as I pulled my phone from my back pocket.

Where are you? - Sarah

My eyes popped wide as I stared down. It was like a bucket of ice water had been thrown on my head, and I pulled away from him.

"Oh my God, I'm sorry. I'm supposed to be somewhere," I said.

"I think that place is right here," Reid said, his hand taking hold of mine.

"No, really. Sarah is downstairs and we have…things. We were headed to food and booze at the Seaside bar in the casino when you distracted me."

"Distracted you? No, you distracted me. You ran into me, remember?" he said with that panty-dropping smirk that tried to entice me to ditch Sarah to stay with those lips of his.

I pulled on his hand, directing him out of the dangerous bedroom and to the door. "Thanks for catching me, by the way."

I paid no attention to anyone else but him as he smiled at me and held the door.

"Anytime. Can I see you again?" he asked, as he walked with me to the elevator.

The door opened, and I stepped on. "Yes!"

The doors slid closed and I fell back against the wall, my hands covering my face as I let out a scream.

What just happened?

CHAPTER THREE

"What the hell took you so long?" Sarah said as I sat down. My mouth popped open, but I didn't know where to begin. I was still in shock over the whole thing. "Wrong elevator."

"And it took you an hour to get back down?"

"Well..."

"Oh my God, just spit it out."

"I ran into Reid Gallagher in the elevator, and we were talking and flirting and he showed me his penthouse suite."

She blinked at me, then her gaze narrowed. "What really happened? Jeremy didn't call you or something and you're just trying to cover it up, right?"

"I said—" I drew in a breath at the feel of hands landing on my hips, a tingle rushing through me as lips brushed against my ear. It set my whole body on fire, and I leaned back into the flames.

"I didn't get your number," Reid said, his voice low and setting off every nerve in my body.

I turned to him and blinked. "You want my number?"

"How else am I going to see you again?"

My mouth dropped open as I remembered the elevator.

Sarah's hand clamped down on my arm, her fingers digging in, but I ignored her.

"You really do want to see me again?" I asked in disbelief.

He backed up, his hands leaving me. "Okay, I totally read the vibes wrong." He gestured behind him. "I'll just be going."

"Wait! No, that's not what I meant. What I meant was—I'd love to see you again."

"Yeah?"

"Yeah."

He beamed at me. "Great, great." He pulled out his phone and I added my number to his contacts list, which had fewer numbers than I expected.

"Oh, shit. Sorry," he said as he looked behind me. "Hi, I'm Reid."

Sarah made a strange uh-huh sound. "Y-yeah. Hi."

"This is my friend, Sarah. She's getting married this weekend."

"Congrats. Are you girls here for some fun before she ties the knot?"

"Actually, the wedding is in the hotel," I said, since Sarah seemed to suddenly be mute.

"Wow, how'd you swing that?" he asked.

"Connections, I hear." I slapped Sarah's hand that was cutting off circulation in my arm. "I tap out. Let go," I hissed.

"Cool. I'll let you get back to your drinks. I've got to be on set tomorrow, but maybe I can see you when I have a break?"

"That would be… Yes."

"She'd love to!" Sarah practically screamed in my ear.

Reid jumped a bit and tried to suppress a chuckle. "Have fun."

"Oh my God. Oh my God. Oh my God!" Sarah was practically hyperventilating as I watched him walk away.

My eyes were glued to his ass. How had I missed it earlier? It was fantastic.

"I know."

"Harp…"

"Yeah."

"He came down to find you to get your number."

I was still so in awe that he asked me for my number that I completely forgot he had to find me in the maze of the casino first.

"He's even more gorgeous in person," Sarah said with a dreamy sigh. "I thought you were pulling my leg. I mean, I know Josh West is here this week, but I didn't expect to see him or any other celebrities."

"They're filming in and around the hotel, I guess. Some new action flick."

"He looked more buff than normal."

She was right. In most roles, Reid was a fit, muscular guy, but not bulky. He was more on the bulky side for whatever he was filming.

"Year made, and it's only January."

"If you have a date with him, that's decade made."

"So true." I held up my glass and clinked it against hers before taking a sip. "We need to find those yards of margaritas."

"What the hell happened? Tell me everything."

And I did, every last detail over multiple drinks.

"Oh, man, his man-ness was like…" I held my arms up. "Man."

Sarah erupted in a fit of giggles. "What about his other man-ness."

"Man, I didn't feel that, but yeah, I'd do him. Totally."

She straightened up, eyes wide. "You have to do him. Like, have to, have to. It's imperative."

"Imperative. Yeah." I let out a groan just remembering the feel of him. "His arms, his chest. He's sculpted and hard and perfect. I could lick him all over." I demonstrated by lapping up the sugar from the rim of my glass.

"That's hot. You need to do that when you see him tomorrow."

"Yeah."

Somewhere in my mind I knew it was all drunk talk, but it still sounded like a good idea.

After finishing our drinks, we grabbed some dinner, which helped to sober us up a little, but I didn't seem to care because I was riding an unexpected high. Meeting Reid, talking to him, was an experience I'd never forget.

"How are you doing?" Sarah asked as she looked over at my machine. "Holy shit!"

I grinned at her almost maniacally. "This machine loves me."

"Are you doing max bet?"

"I'm switching it up, but I was max when I hit that bonus spin and it paid off big time." I was up almost four hundred dollars.

A few hours, a few drinks, and a few hundred dollars won later, Sarah and I made it back to our room.

As I lay in bed, I thought about the amazing day. I couldn't keep the smile from my face all night. It only grew when Sarah recounted everything to Rob via FaceTime when we were at dinner.

"You're still thinking about him, aren't you?" Sarah asked from the other bed.

"Duh."

She chucked a pillow at me. "At least you're smiling again. A real smile, not those fake ones you've been tossing me for months."

My phone pinged, and I picked it up from the nightstand. There was a text from an unfamiliar number.

Goodnight, beautiful – Reid

I sat straight up, my whole body vibrating like I was about to take off.

"What?"

"He texted me. Reid texted me."

She sat up as well. "No shit?"

I handed the phone over to her. "How do I respond? I don't know how to do this!" My voice was in full-out panic. It'd been years since I'd done the whole flirtation thing, and I had no clue how it worked. Even then, Jeremy never gave me the stomach-churning, anxiety-inducing excitement I was feeling. Maybe that should have been my first clue, but I didn't catch on, naïve to what chemistry should be.

And my chemistry with Reid was off the charts. Plus the minor freak out that someone like Reid texted me.

"You definitely have to respond," she said.

"With what?"

"Something light and funny. Think cute."

I stared at her with large, wide eyes. "Thinking cute isn't going to help me."

"Don't be self-deprecating again."

"So just say goodnight back?"

She shook her head and handed the phone back to me. "It needs a little something extra, since he added beautiful."

"Like what? Handsome? Sexy? Need a bed warmer?" I was definitely down for warming his bed.

"Don't let your pussy do the talking. You have to start PG or you'll just be another notch."

"Oh my God. That's what this is, isn't it? Just another girl in a long line." I'd gone from excited panic to heartbroken panic in less than a second. Sure, sleeping with him would be a great memory, but that wasn't all I wanted. Our time together may have been short, but I really liked it.

"Stop. I just said not to do shit like that. You don't know. Didn't you say something about something someone said?"

My brow scrunched, and one side of my top lip raised up. "What nonsense are you spewing?"

She rolled her eyes. "The guy he threw out."

"And?"

"It seemed like Reid's not getting any, and possibly hasn't for a while."

"True." She was right. Reid's mood had flipped like a switch at the comment.

I stared at the screen, willing myself to come up with something clever, but my brain was short circuited as I stared at his message.

Reid-fucking-Gallagher was messaging me!

Goodnight, strong chest – Harper

My fingers flew across the screen and I hit send, then let the phone drop down to the bed as I buried my face in my hands. "That was a shit response. I suck at this."

"Harp…" she trailed off, and my phone buzzed again.

My chest clenched in anticipation as I looked down at the new message.

Strong chest? Is that all I'm good for? – Reid

"You got him talking, keep going," Sarah said in encouragement after I read it to her.

Goodnight, beautiful grey eyes – Harper

"Just tattoo *awkward AF* on my forehead to warn people."

"He's playing with you. Play back."

"I don't know what to say."

It's all about the physical with you, huh? – Reid

Crap, I needed to turn things around.

No, and you started it – Harper

Blame it on the man – Reid

I let out a laugh, my nervousness subsiding a tiny bit.

Of course – Harper

I smiled down at my phone.

"What did he say now?" Sarah asked.

"I think we're flirting." I leaned back against the headboard and waited for his response, which took about five seconds.

Okay, what else? – Reid

Why am I the one fanning your greatness? Don't you have fangirls for that? – Harper

I do, but I like to know what you think of me – Reid

"Oh, he likes you," Sarah gushed as she read the messages. I looked over to her. "How can you tell?"

"Because he's fishing for your attraction to him."

Why me? – Harper

A question I'd been asking since he said he wanted to see me again.

Because I gave you my number, and that means more than you know. I had fun with you and I'd like to get to know you better – Reid

I read it again and again. All the calm I'd gained was gone, and I felt like I was about to hyperventilate.

"I'm about to freak out here," I said, showing Sarah the new messages. "Do those words actually exist, or is that my wishful thinking?"

"If you're talking about him wanting to get to know you, those words are actually there."

"Holy shit." I stared at her.

Her brown eyes were wide as she gave me a stare down. "Girl, you are rolling with this or I'm never talking to you again."

"What?"

"I'm serious. If you let an opportunity with Reid-fucking-Gallagher slip through your fingers, I will never forgive you."

"Harsh much?" I chucked her pillow back at her.

She caught it and tossed it back. "Truth hurts. Now, back to Reid."

I'd like that as well – Harper
Very much.

Good. Now let's continue. Goodnight elevator interloper – Reid

Goodnight hands I w – Harper My eyes widened as I looked down at the screen. I changed my mind and was backing up over the letters when my finger shifted and accidently hit send.

"Shit!"

"What?" Sarah asked. I flashed the phone to her, and she merely shrugged. "It's out there, roll with it."

What hands? – Reid

I'm trying to keep this PG. You weren't supposed to see that – Harper

But I did see it – Reid

Unsee it – Harper

It doesn't work that way – Reid

I really wanted to send a GIF of Tim Gunn and his infamous "Make it work" line, but my phone didn't do GIFs.

I want your hands as well – Reid

My heart slammed in my chest, my thoughts decidedly moving away from PG and straight to X. Heat exploded through my body with the idea of his hands on me.

PG! – Harper

So I can HOLD them. You have such a dirty mind. Tsk-tsk ;) – Reid

I'd like that – Harper

Goodnight Harper. Don't let the bed bugs bite – Reid

Only you – Harper

"Stop bogarting the conversation. I want to looky," Sarah said with a grabby hand.

"Hold please."

"Ugh, you suck."

I smiled down at the screen, ignoring Sarah as I soaked in my conversation with Reid.

What happened to PG? – Reid

I'm really curious about this biting thing. You brought it up. Sweet dreams – Harper

If they're of you they'll be the best dreams I've had in months – Reid

My heart sped up, chest clenching as I wondered if it was all really happening.

What are your plans for tomorrow, accoster? – Reid

I blinked at the screen as the second message popped in, and I turned to Sarah. "What are we doing tomorrow?"

"It's pretty laid back. Some shopping, more of today."

Probably rising too early – Harper

Pretty sure after today that's what I'll be doing – Reid

I'll ignore your non-PG comment, and instead say how you should come find me tomorrow and give me some more of that good luck juju – Harper

Why give me that opening? – Reid

Now who has a dirty mind? I was talking about all the slots winnings I had tonight. Looking for a repeat tomorrow – Harper

More slots? – Reid

After some breakfast and a shower with some shopping in between – Harper

Maybe I'll come find you – Reid

Ooh, are you going to stalk me? – Harper

Maybe. But for now, I'm looking forward to dreams of you – Reid

Goodnight, most amazing man I've ever met – Harper

Now you're just playing me up – Reid

Not to say I don't like it – Reid

Because I do – Reid

My heart felt like it was going to force its way from my chest, sprout wings, and fly away. "What is going on?" I asked Sarah as I handed her the phone.

"You're being chased by the hottest man I've ever seen, and you better ride his pony stick."

"Excuse me? Are you whoring me out?" I asked in mock credulity.

"I'm out of time, so you have to take one for the team."

"Such a hardship."

"Right?"

We both fell back in laughter as we snuggled into bed. The day had gone very differently from what I expected when I woke that morning. I'd been hoping for girl time and Vegas fun. I could never have dreamed up what actually happened.

It was quite possibly the best day of my life.

CHAPTER FOUR

The next morning I awoke from a dream about a Hollywood heartthrob in my bed.

My head was also throbbing, but I didn't get nearly the enjoyment from it as I did my dream guy. I thought I went to bed pretty sober, the alcohol having worked its way through my body, burned off by dancing in the middle of bays of slot machines.

Then again, I was fairly certain we failed to drink enough water. In fact, the only water we'd had was the ice in our drinks.

I pulled my phone from the nightstand and groaned at the time. Damn three-hour difference had me up way too early. So much for us getting on local time when my body was saying, "Get up, bitch, it's after nine." The reality of my location was just after six in the morning.

The sun wasn't even up, for fuck's sake. Why was my brain suddenly perked up when my body was obviously happy to stay snuggled in bed?

The scratch in my throat reminded me and I pawed at the bottle of water I knew was somewhere on the nightstand. Thankfully it was a full bottle, because I think I broke a world record with how fast I chugged it.

Water was life in the desert of my body and I was in desperate need for more. My mind, however, wanted to get back to the dream I was having. I'd been so close to getting fucked by Reid Gallagher.

I was using my phone as a flashlight, scanning the room for a bottle within reaching distance when it buzzed in my hand.

I blinked as I stared at the text message through blurry eyes, my mind unable to process the words.

Rise and shine, beautiful – Reid

Finally they clicked, and I remembered my dream was actually reality.

"Oh my God!" I screamed as I sat straight up.

"Why are you screeching, harpy?" Sarah groaned as she rubbed her face across her pillow.

"Reid texted me." I read it over and over, going back over the other messages and seeing our obvious flirting in texted words.

"And?" Sarah groaned.

"I thought it was all a dream."

"Nope. Now, shh," she whispered, her hand giving the international symbol to lower the volume.

I was transfixed by the memories, my whole body lighting up. The smile on my face refused to be anything less than megawatt.

For the first time in years, I was having fun with a guy. I was even flirting, in my own awkward way. The time we spent together, while short, was also magical in ways I couldn't comprehend. I was pretty sure by the slew of texts in my phone that I wasn't the only one who felt that way.

Rising, but my shine is a little dull. How's your rising?
– Harper

Full now ;) – Reid

I bit my bottom lip and fell back onto the bed, a high-pitched squeal leaving me as I slammed my hands and feet on the bed.

The sudden slam of a pillow at my head stopped me and I grabbed it and snuggled it to my chest as I turned to Sarah. Even her morning crankiness and my hangover couldn't tamp down my excitement.

***

Some room service, a couple of gallons of water, and a hot shower later, we were back with the land of the living and back down to the call of the pretty-pretty lights.

The slots were *not* being kind to me today. They were downright mean. I was down two hundred dollars for the day, a lot of my winnings from the night before after riding my Reid high gone. The one good thing was that the stack of cash I'd brought for gambling hadn't diminished—yet.

"How's it going?" Sarah asked, popping up behind me and way too chipper considering how I'd felt that morning.

"You're going to get the hotel's signature notepad as a wedding gift," I said with a sigh.

She pulled on my arm. "Come on, let's go over there."

"Are the sparkly lights calling you?"

"Yes."

Somehow Sarah had this sense. I could swear the machines called to her. She'd put in five dollars and get twenty. I would play the machine next to her and lose forty in the same time frame.

I stood in front of a machine, refusing to sit because I'd commit to feeding it more money just to get the bonus game.

A gasp escaped at the shock of hands on my hips that exploded up and around my body.

"Hey, stranger," a familiar voice tickled my ear.

That voice. Smooth, deep, with a slight gruffness at times. It was enough to make my knees go weak, and I might have fallen if it wasn't for him holding me up.

I turned to find Reid smiling at me, and found a similar grin forming on my lips. "Hey." I glanced around and spotted two guys about ten feet away seeming to be with him. "What are you doing here?"

"I was walking through and spotted you."

I wasn't sure I believed that he was just walking through, not with the couple of guys hanging back a good ten feet escorting him. Or maybe I just wanted to believe he was seeking me out.

"Are you done filming?"

He shook his head. "On a lunch break, but I wanted to give you this." He handed me one of the hotel room keys that looked a lot like my own, only it was gold and not the aqua color of mine.

"What's this?" I asked as I held it up.

"A key to my room."

My eyes widened. "You're giving me a key to your room? How do you know I'm not a complete psycho who will use it to come over in the middle of the night and take advantage of you?"

That sexy, wolfish grin spread on his lips. "I can't say I'm opposed to that. At all. Take all the advantage you want."

I couldn't help biting down on my lower lip, heat spreading through my cheeks. "What am I really doing with this?"

"I want to see you later, but it won't be until later in the afternoon. I can text you, and if you're free, just come on up." He pointed to the key in my hand. "You need it for the elevator."

"Oh, right." Something I would never forget.

"Does that sound good?" he asked, suddenly not as confident as he did moments before.

"Hmm?"

His brow knit and his lips formed a thin line. "It doesn't exactly sound the best."

I thought back on what he said. "Coming when you call?"

"Yeah."

"Honestly, I'll take any time I can get, so I'll gladly be your beck and call girl."

"Ha! How did I know you'd take it there?"

I shrugged my shoulders. "Sixth sense? Proficiency in perverted thoughts?"

"That must be it."

"Anyway, we're going down the strip as soon as Sarah finishes off that twenty, but we should be back mid-afternoon." I was going to make damn sure we were, and I knew Sarah would as well.

"Excellent," he said as he leaned forward, his lips pressing against mine.

A gasp left me and heat flooded me at the brief contact.

"Sorry," he said as he pulled back. "I couldn't help myself."

I wrapped my arms around his neck and pulled him down to me, our lips meeting again. I needed to double check what I felt, but the second time I was totally wrong.

It was more. My whole body bowed into him as his presence intoxicated my blood. It went from our lips pressed together to his arms around me, holding me close as his tongue caressed mine.

"Holy moly," I said when he pulled back.

"I...damn, girl." His eyes were a darker shade of grey, and he didn't release his arms from me. "Where did you come from?"

"Was I in your dreams last night?" I asked.

"Yes."

"That's where."

He let out a sigh and pressed his forehead to mine. "You don't understand how true I'm beginning to believe that is."

"Reid, we need to go," one of the guys called.

It was then I noticed we'd gathered a bit of an audience, and I saw a few phones out.

Great.

"This afternoon?" he asked.

I nodded. "I can't wait."

He beamed at me and placed a kiss to my forehead before tearing his arms from me and holding them high in the air as he walked away backwards.

"Gotta deactivate my magnets before the pull is too great and I never let you go."

I threw my head back and laughed. "You're so extra."

"Extra what?"

"I haven't figured it out yet."

"You let me know first thing," he said with a wink. "Later, beautiful."

"Later, man of my dreams."

He threw his fist in the air in a *Breakfast Club* way. "Now that's what I'm talking about."

"What did I miss?" Sarah said, popping up beside me, her gaze glued to Reid's retreating form.

"Did we die in a plane crash on the way over here?" I asked.

"I don't think so. Why?"

"Because I can't figure out if that man is heaven or hell, but he's definitely not real life." Pain shot through my forearm, and I winced as I rubbed at the spot Sarah just pinched. "What the hell?"

"You're not dreaming. That man really does want you. Lucky bitch."

***

I'm back. Not much time, but if you're free, I'm here –
Reid

I stared down at my phone, my stomach in knots as my skin vibrated. At least that was what it felt like.

"He's back," I said to Sarah. I bent over and blew out a breath. "I think I'm going to be sick."

We'd headed to the outlet mall after Reid left and spent a few hours there before returning to the hotel for some food and more gambling.

"You're going to be fine," she assured me. "Just breathe, and remember how his lips felt on yours. Go get that man."

"Why do I feel like your sexual science experiment?"

"Because you are. But besides that, I haven't seen you like this since Will in college. He was really interested in you, but you never acted on it and lost out, and that was only a fraction of what I see right now."

"Yeah, well, Will was my league. Reid is so many levels above me."

"Stop selling yourself short!" she Fuck Jeremy for making you doubt you could be the one for someone. He was a fucker who used you. Reid's different."

"How do you know?"

"Blind faith. Now go to that man, and report back after you've drained him."

"I'm not fucking him right now!" My eyes popped wide. "Wait. Do you think that was what he meant by all this?"

Sarah sighed, turned me around, and pushed. "Stop overthinking shit."

Anxiety spiked with each step, my heart beating wildly as I drew in gulping breaths. What was I doing? I hit the button and closed my eyes as I waited.

Sarah was right. I had to get over the insecurities Jeremy left with me, but saying and doing were two totally different things. Nothing would change unless I initiated change, and going up to Reid's room was the first step.

The doors slid open, and I stepped in. With shaking hands, I pulled the card from my back pocket and waved it in front of the receiving pad. The numbers lit up, and I pressed the button for the penthouse floor.

I was worth more. I was worth a man giving me more than words and false sincerity. I deserved a chance to dive into whatever was happening with Reid.

When the elevator slowed, my nerves spiked again. Each step was ghostly, like something else was driving my body closer. I reached out and knocked.

A minute later, the door swung open and I blew out a breath of relief at the blonde who answered. There were people, which meant no sex.

Probably.

"Who are you?" the blonde asked snidely.

I was taken aback as all of Reid's people had been super nice. Even Kiki with her protective edge wasn't like the woman in front of me.

"Um, hi. I'm Harper."

"Who?"

"Reid is expecting me," I explained.

"No, he's not." She started to close the door, but I stepped forward.

"Yes, he is," I said as I attempted to move past her.

She stepped in front of me, blocking the way. "You're not getting in."

"Fine." I pulled out my phone and texted Reid. The chick rolled her eyes and slammed the door in my face.

Some bitch won't let me through the door – Harper

Once it was sent, I pulled the key Reid had given me from my back pocket and waved it in front of the door. Why that hadn't occurred to me in the first place I blamed totally on my mini freak out. The click sounded, and I turned the handle and pushed the door open. Bitch's eyes widened as she gasped in shock.

"You fucking psycho! Deon, call security!" she called over her shoulder.

I flashed the key at her. "You can't open the door without a key, you stupid bitch." Of all the things trying to keep me from him, she wasn't going to be one of them.

"I can't believe you went that far, you fucking stalker," she spat.

"Excuse me?" I'd never been in a fight before, but if she kept it up, that could change.

"Oh, damn. Reid, you better get out here," the guy I was guessing to be Deon called out.

"Why?" I heard him say from the bedroom area, and I watched him come out, pulling a T-shirt over his head. I was glued to his six-pack, how his muscles rippled with any movement.

Sex with this man? Yes, please.

"I will rip every hair from your scalp if you don't get the fuck out of here," the blonde spat, drawing my attention back to her.

"Who the fuck said you could talk to my guest like that, Jenn?" Reid growled.

The blonde's eyes popped open and then suddenly morphed. "Reid, this girl tried to break into your room. I was only trying to stop her." I nearly gagged at the bubbly fakeness of her voice. Talk about two-faced.

Reid's eyes narrowed on her. "Get out."

She whipped around to me, a wicked smile on her face. "You hear—"

"I was talking to you, Jenn," he interrupted her.

She blinked at him. "What?"

"Get. The. Fuck. Out." He was pissed now. My thighs clenched at the sound, and I felt heat surge to my face when his eyes locked onto mine. The man did things to me without

- 45 -

even trying. "Go back to your room and stay there until you can act like a fucking human."

She didn't move, just stared at him. "Reid."

He stepped forward, into my personal space, and grabbed onto my waist. With a tug, I slammed against his chest. "Hi."

I smiled up at him. "Hi."

"I've got an hour laid out for just the two of us."

"That doesn't seem nearly long enough."

"It's not, but it's what I have." He turned and looked at the blonde who was staring at us. "You're still here? Go to your room, Jenn."

"But—" she tried to say something, but Reid cut her off again.

"Deon," Reid called out. The man I'd marked as Deon stood and headed over. He was imposing and it only increased with each step.

"Yes, sir," Deon said.

"Can you please escort Jenn out and revoke her access to my room?"

Deon nodded. "Of course."

"Wait, you can't do that," she argued.

"Says who?" Reid glared at her.

I watch as Deon ushered the still-gaping blonde out the door. As soon as she was gone, Reid turned his attention back to me. "Now, where were we?"

"Wow," I said, still amazed by the way things had gone down.

"Wow, what?"

"Remind me not to get on your bad side."

He laughed at that. "You don't have to worry. She was already hanging by a thread, being clingy and possessive like

I was going to fuck her the second we were alone and she could seduce me, which would have been never."

"That's reserved for me," I said in a low voice, hoping for confirmation.

"Hell, yes." He beamed at me.

"Who is she? I mean, why do you keep her around?"

"She won't be anymore. It's only been a week, and I'm fucking sick of her. The studio assigned her as an assistant for the movie."

"Studio-assigned assistant?" I asked.

"She does the menial tasks that my assistant doesn't have time for."

"Like?" I asked. His whole world was so new and interesting to me.

"Get my protein shakes, grab something I left in the room. She's a gopher."

I furrowed my brow. "Did you just call her a gopher?"

"Yeah. Go. For."

"I seriously thought you just called her a rodent," I said as the laugh left me.

"My dad always twists words and sayings. I was chief gopher as a kid. Had the shirt and all."

"Pics or it didn't happen."

He let out a laugh and pulled out his phone.

"You have it on your phone?" I asked as I peeked over at his screen.

"No, but I'll have my mom find it."

I blinked at him. "Really?"

"Really."

It seemed an awful lot to do just for me, some random woman.

"Who is your normal assistant?" I asked, trying not to think too hard about a deeper meaning.

"Oh, shit." His eyes went wide like he'd forgotten something and turned his head. "Yo, Tre."

The dark-skinned man from across the room held up his finger as he typed furiously on his laptop and spoke into a bluetooth earpiece. After a minute, he finished up and walked over.

"You've got makeup in thirty, and Josh wants to go over the argument scene again."

Reid nodded. "Okay. Now, say hi to Harper."

Recognition sparked in Tre's eyes, and he gave me a wide smile and held out his hand. "Hey, nice to meet you, Harper. Someone can't stop talking about you."

I shook his hand and gave a shy smile. "He's not the only one."

"You can't stop talking about you, too?"

My eyes went wide. "N-no, I meant…" My face felt like it was on fire, and I avoided looking at Reid from embarrassment. "I can't stop thinking about him either." I shot a quick glance over to Reid, and my heart nearly exploded from the smile on his face.

"Well, I said talking, but that's about the same as thinking for Reid," Tre said, ribbing his boss whose mouth was dropped open.

"Really, man? I should fire you for that shit," Reid said, but there was no malice in his tone.

"I'd like to see you try," Tre countered with a smirk, making it obvious it was a normal back and forth for them.

"I could do it," Reid argued.

"Right. Keep telling yourself you could function without me. In the meantime, I'll be over there organizing your shit show of a schedule."

"Speaking of, did you do it?" Reid asked.

Tre nodded. "Yeah, you pain in the ass, it's done."

"Thanks. We're going to go upstairs."

Tre nodded in understanding. "Have fun."

Reid's fingers caressed my palm before slipping between mine. "Come on."

"Where are we going?"

"It's a surprise."

He led us out into the hall and the elevator, but instead of pressing the button to go down, he pressed up. I hadn't even noticed it as the penthouse button had been larger than the rest, but above that sat an R symbol. A short trip up, a few steps, and the concrete walls opened up to a large rooftop deck. Plush outdoor couches were speckled around along with some glass tables. There was even a small pool, but it was closed.

We walked up to the glass railing and leaned onto the edge. The drop wasn't far, the upper deck only taking up a portion of the roof, so that was comforting.

My mouth dropped open as I looked out at the awe-inspiring view. "Wow." The entire strip could be seen, all the way down to the airport. The mountains circled all around, standing much taller than the roof we stood on.

"Nice, isn't it?" he asked.

"Amazing. A perk of having the penthouse?"

"Yep. Only the upper floors have access."

We stood there just looking out. A breeze blew by and a shiver rolled through me. Reid wrapped his arm around my shoulder and rubbed my arm to warm it.

"You and Tre seem close." The vibe was not the typical boss and employee.

He nodded. "He's been working for me for almost a decade. I trust him more than anyone else."

"I bet that's a hard thing."

"It is. That's why I have a tight circle."

"I've watched you throw two people out of your room," I pointed out.

"There's my inner circle, and then there's the outer circle. The inner circle wouldn't pull some of this shit those two did. For one, the inner folks already know about you. They're the people I trust the most and are closest to me in my life. They're my ride or die."

"What do they know about me?"

"About how I'm interested in this random chick I met in an elevator. They got a kick out of it."

My heart leapt at his interested comment, but I tried to play it off and not show my excitement. "Did you tell them your magnet story?"

"Hell, yes. I'm using that as our official meeting."

Another gust of wind whipped by, and he guided us over to sit on one of the couches.

While his room held a small handful of people, the day before had been bustling. "Do you normally travel with such an entourage?"

He shook his head. "No. I had a little downtime over the weekend, so I brought some friends out for the opening. Everyone today is because they're necessary."

"That's a lot of necessity." I'd counted at least three people, and only one had been one of the escorts when he found me in the casino.

"There's a lot that goes into making a movie. Many moving parts you never see."

I turned back to admire the landscape. "That would be cool to see some time."

"I can arrange it. Just tell me when."

"I may take you up on that, but first, can I ask you a question?" It was something that had been bothering me since our texting the night before. Something I needed to clear up.

"As many as you want."

"Am I just another conquest?" I asked.

He blew out a breath. "I get why you're asking, and the honest answer is no. You aren't some battle to win and move past to the next. I don't play those games. I won't say I never did, though, but I was a lot younger then, and fame was new. Pussies rained like confetti, and they still do, but that's not what I'm looking for."

"What are you looking for?" I asked.

"Something more. Someone I can talk to and laugh with. Someone where I'm not Reid Gallagher superstar, but just Reid," he elaborated. "I want to be myself, not some image."

"It's lonely, huh?" It was an interesting insight. The more he divulged, the more I felt for him. A beautiful bird in a gilded cage.

"It can be," he confirmed. "Constantly surrounded by people, but not knowing who to trust and who is just out to use you."

I slipped my fingers between his. "Well, I'm happy to get to know you."

"Don't misunderstand, though," he said, twisting his arm to raise my hand. His lips pressed against my palm before lowering it back down. "I'm very attracted to you, but I'm not using this as a way to get you to bed."

I nodded. "Good to know. There are much simpler ways to accomplish that."

"Oh yeah? What are those?"

Every scenario I'd thought about since the moment I met him circulated through my mind.

"Picking me up and throwing me on the bed, then ripping my clothes off would be perfectly acceptable."

He let out a groan and leaned back against the couch. "You're killing me."

"Sorry. Somehow you make my body go into overdrive," I said with a shrug.

"Have dinner with me tomorrow."

"Dinner?" The invitation was so sudden I was caught off guard.

"Somewhere that isn't so close to a bed where we can talk more without temptation, because I can throw Tre and the others out right now and we can go back and do that. Trust me, it's tempting."

I worried my bottom lip. "Sorry. Nervousness makes me blurt out embarrassing thoughts."

"It's adorable. Now, back to dinner."

I racked my brain trying to remember what was going on. Sarah would push me to agree no matter what, but when I remembered Rob was coming in that night, it was quite perfect. They needed some alone time when he arrived, and therefore I would be alone anyway.

"I'd love to."

He blew out a breath, a dazzling smile lighting up his face. "Great."

"Were you nervous I'd say no?" I asked, and he gave a nod. "Seriously? Say no to a date with the most gorgeous man I've ever met? You're crazy."

He leaned in, his gaze boring into me. "I want to kiss you."

"What's stopping you?"

"Fear."

I blinked at him. "Of me?"

His hand slipped up my neck, sending tingles cascading across my skin. "Of not being able to stop because I learned early it's even more perfect than I'd fantasized. You're special, and I'm not bullshitting you."

My heart hammered against my breastbone, hard and fast. "You barely know me."

"I know, but I'm going with my gut, and it's telling me to chase you."

"That's constipation."

He chuckled. "Seriously, though, I feel like there could be something here. You're worth the chase."

"Am I?"

His brow furrowed as he studied me. "Someone really fucked with your head, didn't they?"

I looked down to my lap as I fidgeted with the hem of my shirt. "It's not just that."

"But I'm right."

"That's beside the point."

"What is the point?" he asked.

I tore myself away from him, standing to walk back over to the railing. "I'm just an average person living an average life in Ohio. You're an international superstar."

He stepped up beside me. "Who once upon a time was an average boy living an average life in Ohio. Probably only a couple of miles from you."

"That's kinda unbelievable. To be so close and to have never met." How many instances had we been in the same place at the same time?

"You never know, we could have met. What year did you graduate?"

"2008. You?"

"Well, I was in L.A. at the time, but 2004."

At least I roughly knew his age to be around thirty-two.

A ringing made up both jump and he pulled out his phone. "Yeah?" he said as he answered. "Okay, I'm coming." He blew out a breath as he hung up the phone. "Time's up."

"That was way too fast," I said as we headed back to the elevator.

"Agreed," he said as he took my hand, giving it a squeeze. "Have fun tonight."

"You, too."

We stepped into the elevator and he hit the buttons for the penthouse and the lobby. "I'll probably be doing stunts until three in the morning."

"Then dreaming about our date."

"Damn straight." The door opened and he straddled the opening and pulled me close, placing a kiss to my forehead. "Goodnight, beautiful."

He reluctantly pulled away, his gaze never leaving mine until the doors closed.

More than excitement coursed through me. It was a lightness in my chest, a feeling I'd long ago forgotten. It was the high of attraction, and it was euphoric.

CHAPTER FIVE

"You are my idol," Sarah said the moment my eyes cracked open. She was snuggled in, choking out another pillow as she waited for me to wake up, a creepy-ass smile on her face.

I groaned. "I can't believe this is happening."

"Believe it. Reid-fucking-Gallagher will be at this door tonight to sweep you off your feet. Just don't forget us little people when you're living it up."

I couldn't tell who was more excited about my date—me or Sarah.

"What the fuck are you talking about?"

"You know, when you move to Hollywood to be with him. Don't forget your bestie braving the cold Ohio winters."

I scoffed and threw a pillow at her. "It's a date."

"Uh huh. I've seen the smitten looks you throw each other."

"So? That doesn't mean anything. All that says is we haven't fucked."

"If that was it, he'd have nothing but lust in his eyes, and there is more than that. You got to him."

After leaving Reid the day before, I returned to our room and Sarah descended. Question after question. It was an inquisition, and she wanted every last detail and answers I didn't have. In the end, I bribed her with a show to stop talking about it because she was sending me into full panic mode. I was already nervous enough. I didn't need to be revved up even more.

I even sweetened the pot by suggesting one of two shows I knew Rob wouldn't go to—*Australia's Thunder From Down Under* or *Backstreet Boys*. With the way things were going and her attachment to my current love life pop-up, it wasn't much of a surprise that she picked the hunks.

"Even if that's true, I leave on Sunday, remember?"

"Stop being a pessimist."

"It's not pessimistic to be a realist. I like him, really I do, but reality is a stuck-up baseball player's shoulder, a whiny fifteen-year-old basketball player who doesn't want to do the work, and three new patients on Monday."

"Does that asshole still think he's God's gift to women?" she asked with a roll of her eyes.

I sat up with my legs crossed and hugged my pillow. "Yes. Can you believe he told me to fly back on our normal days to get his sessions in?"

"There's like five other therapists there," she said.

"Exactly, and Andy took him on, but that didn't make him happy because Andy's a guy."

"Doesn't he have like an in-house therapist?" she asked.

I nodded. "He's down for the season so they sent him to us."

"Here's an idea. You could become Reid's personal therapist."

My expression dropped, and I gave her my best resting bitch face. "Let's see if he still has interest in me after tonight, and then you can plan the rest of my life out."

"Oh, he's going to fall head over heels for you. I can feel it."

I twirled my hand in the air. "That's just your lady bits missing Rob."

"That too," she said with a wag of her eyebrows.

"When does he get in?" I asked, thinking about our schedule.

"Around six."

That gave us roughly ten hours to run errands and have some fun before she checked into their room.

"What am I going to wear?" I asked, eyes wide. With years separating my last first date, I didn't have a clue how things went.

She threw the covers off her and sat up. "Casual or dress up?"

I stared blankly at her. "I have no idea."

Her arms stretched high above her head. "Better to ask, then we can buy you a first date outfit to drive him crazy."

"I brought plenty of clothes."

"But no *first date with Reid Gallagher* clothes."

I pulled out my phone and shot him a text.

Morning, handsome. What's the dress code for tonight? – Harper

Whatever you want or nothing at all – Reid

What happened to PG? – Harper

Morning wood and your name on my screen – Reid

My eyes widened as I stared down at my phone. Reid's body was hard, taut, and suddenly all I could think about was another part of his anatomy with that same description.

Sorry – Reid

But not really – Reid

"What?" Sarah asked, and I realized I was gaping down at the words.

"He's hard."

Sarah scrambled over to me, her expression bordering on manic. "Did you just get a dick pic?" The excitement fell from her face as she looked down at the screen. "Damn, I was really hoping it was a dick pic."

Me, too. Though not really. I wanted to see it, but unsolicited dick pics were not cool. Barely two days had passed since I'd crashed into him, but it felt like it was a longer period of time.

Uh oh, did I lose you? – Reid

Oh! No. My brain just stopped at morning wood – Harper

Rebooting – Harper

Ha! Let me turn this off so you can turn it back on later – Reid

And it's Vegas. We can swing casual to black tie, whatever you want – Reid

Kind of a dressy casual? I'm just imagining you in jeans and a button down with the sleeves rolled up and the top buttons undone – Harper

Just like the day we met.

I can definitely do that – Reid

Any requests? – Harper

I don't care what you wear, I'll just be happy to be near you – Reid

I couldn't help the huge grin on my face.

Ditto – Harper

It felt good, freeing, to flirt again. I'd forgotten the high that went along with someone showing interest in me.

"Dressy casual," I called out to Sarah who had moved to the bathroom.

She popped out, brush in hand. "You've got some great ass jeans with you. Now we just need to find you a top because I know you didn't bring anything with you."

"Ass jeans?"

"Make your ass look banging."

I rolled my eyes and slid off the bed. "I did bring things."

"Not for a date with Reid Gallagher," she stressed.

"I'm dreaming, aren't I? Like, did I die? Or am I in some catatonic state? That has to be it, right?"

Sarah grabbed onto my arms and looked me dead in the eye. "Reid Gallagher is taking you on a date in real fucking life. So, while we're picking up some things I need for the wedding, we're also going to find you a top."

"What is it you need again?" I asked as I followed her into the bathroom.

"Some Vegas-themed stuff for the guest gift bags. And said bags. I'm hoping to find something in Miracle Mile Shops and maybe The Forum Shops at Caesars Palace. Either way, lots of options."

Room service breakfast and an hour later, we headed down to the lobby to catch a cab. We were quite a few hotels away from where she wanted to go.

"What's wrong with the stores on this end?" I asked as I pulled my sunglasses on. It may have been cool outside, but the sun was still blazing.

"We stayed at Elara last time, and I remember there being a few good souvenir shops in Miracle Mile Shops."

We started there, and I was surprised by the complete circular pattern the mall made. After around twenty shirts were tried on and bags of baubles were purchased, we headed over to The Forum Shops at Caesars Palace.

I stared down the long hall, stores on either side and stories tall. "This is going to take forever."

"Come on." She tugged on my hand.

It took a few stores before we seemed to hit the jackpot of a dozen possibilities.

"What about a halter top?" Sarah asked, scouring the racks.

"It's like forty out," I reminded her. It may have been Vegas, but it was still January.

"Your weather app needs to update. There's a heatwave today and it's like seventy out. Besides, you'll probably be inside."

"Still not warm enough for a halter top."

She rolled her eyes at me. "I've got that cute black cardigan you can borrow."

It was cute and would help keep me warm wherever we went. "Fine," I relented, glowering at the smug smile on her face as she pulled the garment from the rack.

"You're a medium, right?"

I nodded. "Pretty much."

"Now this could be something," Sarah said, her eyes alight.

My eyes narrowed as I glared at the bodysuit Sarah held out in front of her. "You've got to be kidding me."

"Not at all. You're trying it on."

"It's a no," I argued, even though it would get me nowhere. I was her resident try-on doll, after all. Whenever we went shopping, she was always throwing clothes at me to try on.

Sometimes what looked like a cute garment on the rack had us busting out in laughter at how bad it turned out to be.

"It's a yes."

I shook my head. "There is no hiding all the flaws in that thing." It was made for size two women who had zero body fat.

"Shut up and try it on."

"I hate you."

"You love me. Stop fighting it."

She went with me into the dressing room, and I took my clothes off before pulling the offending item up.

The color was a soft red, like terra cotta, with white birds flying around. There was a keyhole peep of my cleavage with a little bow around my neck and a cap sleeve. It was tight around my waist, and the thong was settled between my ass cheeks. I slid my jeans up and buttoned them, and glanced at my reflection before cursing Sarah for being right. My jeans weren't too tight creating the dreaded muffin-top look, and it actually accentuated my curves in all the right ways.

Sarah clapped her hands together, a huge grin on her face. "It's perfect! Cute and sexy, especially with your Mary Jane wedges."

"I hate you," I reiterated.

"You only hate that I was right and you were wrong, and you need to just accept that my fashion is on point."

I moved around in the suit, watching the way it would bunch, hoping to find some flaw, but there was none. She was right. It was perfect.

***

Lunch, some light gambling, and a few hours later we were back in the room, and I was freshly showered. My whole body vibrated, butterflies tumbling in my stomach. I still couldn't believe what was happening, what I was officially getting ready for.

Sarah helped with my hair and makeup, making sure it was on point before I poured myself into the bodysuit. I had to be braless due to the design, and when I clipped the neck piece I felt oddly exposed. The suit acted not only as my top but my only undergarments, and it felt strange.

It didn't help that there was only a thin piece of cloth between my legs.

I turned to Sarah, the whole outfit on. "So?"

"Cute but sexy. Casual but dressy. I think you're good for just about anything he comes up with."

"I can't believe I let you talk me into this thing."

"It's the perfect combo, and you look banging in it. Reid isn't going to be able to resist you."

"You mean he's not going to be able to stop staring at my braless cleavage peeking out from the keyhole cut." I pointed to the skin peeking out. I liked to wear V-neck shirts, but this was situated lower than normal and highlighted the curve of my breasts.

"That, too." She threw her cardigan toward me, then continued to pack her clothes in her suitcase and zipped it up before moving to the bathroom to gather up her toiletries.

"It's riding up my ass," I complained as I picked up the cardigan and set it next to my purse.

"Get over it."

"I hate thongs!"

"Deal with it," she said with a smack on my ass as she passed by to the desk. "Now, I'm headed out to pick up Rob. You have a fantastic night with Reid, and I can't wait to hear all about it in the morning. Check in every once in a while, and I expect you to be gone all night."

"Not that you'll be here when I get back," I pointed out. Her nights with me were over once Rob checked in.

"True. I'll be in Rob's room hopefully with him between my thighs, just like you'll be with Reid."

"Great. Thanks. Now I'm getting performance anxiety. I haven't had sex in eight months, remember?"

"It's like riding a bike. Plus, it's got to be better than a guy who just used you to get off on the regular. I mean, have you seen those muscles? I bet he's got the skills." She leaned in and gave me a hug. "Please have fun tonight, and stay safe, okay?"

I nodded. "Be safe, too. Text me when you get back."

With a wave and a blown kiss, she headed out the door.

CHAPTER SIX

Sarah made sure I was presentable and ready to go before she left, so I had time to spare. For twenty minutes, I stewed in anxiety as I waited for Reid.

I popped in a mint, even though I'd just brushed my teeth, and spritzed myself with some more perfume, hoping it wasn't too much. I was adjusting and readjusting and nitpicking everything when there was a sudden knock on the door.

I blew out a steadying breath, my stomach turning, then opened the door.

"Hi," he said when the door opened.

"Wow." He was freshly shaved and smelled divine even from feet away. Per my request, he was in a grey button-down that matched his eyes, the sleeves rolled up his forearms and the top button undone. I stared down at the bundle of brightly colored blossoms. "For me?"

He looked down at his hand and then presented them. "You look...wow. I mean, I already thought you were beautiful, but damn."

I took hold of them, smelling them as I brushed my hair behind my ear and looked to the ground, heat exploding in my cheeks. "Thank you." I stepped back to let him through. "Come on in. I've just got to finish up."

I'd wasted so much time on finalizing my look that I'd forgotten to get my purse together.

"So what are our plans for the evening?" I asked as I tossed my ID, some cash, a credit card, and lipstick into a small crossbody purse with a chain strap. Basically a wristlet with a strap that held the necessities.

"The Tournament of Kings awaits us, m'lady," he said as he propped the flowers up against the wall in a glass from the bathroom.

"Are you serious?" I asked in surprise, grabbing Sarah's cardigan.

"What? It's good, clean, family-friendly, PG-13 fun. Then we can end the evening with a private make-out session in the High Roller while we look at all the lights. What do you think?"

It was not the over-the-top Hollywood date I was expecting, and I liked that. It was different, a little bit silly, but it sounded like casual fun, and more memorable than some expensive display of wealth.

"I think it sounds perfect." I double-checked for my key before shutting the door.

"Yeah?" he asked as we walked down to the elevator.

I nodded. "Just don't tell Sarah we went. She'll pout."

"Her fiancé came in today, right?"

"His plane is due in soon. She went to pick him up."

"So that's where she is," he said as we stepped onto a just-arriving elevator.

"She helped me get ready, and then was out."

There were a few people in the car heading down as well. Every one of them was staring wide-eyed at Reid. I had a feeling that was how the night was going to go.

We got out of the elevator and started to walk when he stopped. "Shit, I left my wallet upstairs," Reid said as he patted his pockets as if it would suddenly appear.

"Is this some trick to get me up to your room?"

He gave me that panty-melting grin again. "I swear, totally unplanned. We're going to have dinner. I guess I just got a little excited about a real old-fashioned date."

"Seriously? You?"

"Believe it or not, I don't go on many. I've been looking forward to it all day. And now I sound like an idiot."

I shook my head no. "I like it."

We walked over to the elevator for the upper floors, and luckily the car was there waiting. I squeezed his hand as the doors closed, and he squeezed back. I watched the screen as floor numbers flew by five at a time, my ears popping around the twentieth floor.

The car suddenly shook and I reached out to steady myself, my hands landing on Reid's bicep and chest. For a second panic surged through me. The elevator screeched to a sudden, shuddering stop, and the lights cut out. Everything was dark, it was complete and total blackness.

For those heartbeats, I wondered if the elevator had plummeted and we were dead, but that thought ended when a dim emergency light flickered on.

Speechless, we stood there trying to figure out what just happened. A strange warmth seeped into my skin, and I realized I wasn't the only one who reached out. One of Reid's arms was around my waist, the other sat on my hip.

"What's going on?" I asked.

"Shh, it's okay," he whispered into my ear, his arm around my waist. "Are you okay?"

"Mm hmm. Just a bit freaked out." Even as I pulled away, I was still latched onto his arm. "What was that?"

"Not sure," he said, his arm leaving my death grip as he stepped over to the control panel and hit the button to open the doors, but nothing happened.

He tried the emergency button, and still nothing.

"That's weird."

More than weird. "I'm calling Sarah," I said as I pulled out my phone and dialed her number.

As with the buttons, nothing happened, just an error message. "What the hell?" I pulled my phone back, looked at the screen, and my stomach dropped. "I have no signal. No phone or data."

"Let me try." His face suddenly lit up from the brightness of his screen, and I watched as a deep crease formed between his brows. "Not good. I have no signal either."

"What's going on?"

"Do you remember what floor we were passing? Was it past fifty?"

"Forty was the last number I remember."

He let out a hard sigh. "Fuck."

"Why?"

"High-speed elevator. It doesn't have an opening until fifty," he explained.

"You mean…" I trailed off. We didn't have a door. There was no opening.

"If it's a power outage, there are backup generators in all these hotels," I said.

"Yeah," he agreed, but there was something in his voice that didn't reassure me.

"But?"

He turned his attention back to me. "Huh?"

"Your tone says you're not sure."

His lips formed a thin line and he seemed to be studying my face. "I don't want to scare you. You don't like elevators, do you?"

I swallowed hard and shook my head. "As long as I try not to think about where we are, I'm okay."

"Okay, that and I don't want to scare myself," he admitted.

"Fine, say it so we can get the freak-out over with."

"The generators for these places kick on automatically."

"And?" I pressed.

"And it's been five minutes," he said.

It felt like my whole body was vibrating. "And?"

"They are set up to turn on within something like a thirty-second window."

"Oh, shit." I bent over and tried to remember the breathing technique my brother used when he had a panic attack. "So, you're saying we're stuck in an elevator with no power and no way out?"

"Basically. But I can't see the power being out long."

I racked my brain trying to come up with any explanation. "It's a new building. Do you think they fucked something up?"

"I would say yes, but no phone signal worries me."

"You always lose signal in elevators," I argued, but by the faint light illuminating his features, I knew it was just me grasping at straws. I fell down onto the floor, my heart jumping into my throat as the car gave a shake.

"It's okay," he assured me and squatted beside me. I realized the squeak I heard came from me. "I'm sure it'll be back on any minute."

"Yeah, you're right." I leaned back against the wall, my knees pulled up to my chest.

Reid relaxed back as well, his long legs crossed out in front of him.

My eyes adjusted to the dim light, but it gave little comfort.

"Look at it this way—you will never forget this first date."

I let out a laugh, long and full. "You really know how to show a girl a good time," I said as I swept tears of laughter and fright from my eyes.

"Let's play twenty questions," he suggested, his hand finding mine and threading our fingers together.

The warmth felt good, and I focused on that and away from the emptiness below us.

"Okay. Not like we can do much else. There's no way out of here until the power comes back."

"Hmm."

"Hmm, what?"

"Is that your first question?" he asked.

I shrugged. "I guess." It wasn't going to be, but he kept drifting off, making me curious as to what he was thinking.

"I was wondering if there was another way out. My turn. What's your last name?"

I let out a hmph. "Going basic."

"I'm saving the more interesting questions for later."

"Evans."

"Evans," he repeated with a nod. "Harper Evans. Good name."

"Is Reid Gallagher your real name?" I asked, thinking back to a few days earlier. "Kalvin alluded it wasn't."

"Yes and no," he said as he shifted his position. "It's technically Arthur Reid Gallagher, but I've gone by Reid since

I was a kid. I hated Art. How long was your last relationship, and when did it end?"

My expression dropped and even in the dark, he noticed.

"Three years, and it ended five months ago. I've been, I don't know, trying to remember who I am since it ended. Same question to you."

He slipped his hand into mine. "I think you have a pretty good handle on who you are."

"Maybe, but I was defined as 'Jeremy's girlfriend' for so many years that the fallout hit me harder than I expected."

"What happened?"

"You still haven't answered my question," I reminded him, hoping to steer the conversation away from my relationship with Jeremy.

"I will, I just don't want you to dodge this conversation. I kinda have you trapped," he pointed out.

I let out a laugh. "In more ways than one, it seems." I ran my hand through my hair and blew out a breath. "Have you ever been with someone, convinced you loved them, you know them, and suddenly they tell you it's over?" He nodded. "Turns out I was just a placeholder. Someone to keep his bed warm until he found Miss Right. He never wanted a future with me. Said we were friends with benefits. I mean, I should have seen it coming. We lived together but it seemed oddly compartmentalized, and talks about the future never went anywhere. I was just too stupid to see all the signs."

He squeezed my hand. "They say love is blind. It can force you to rationalize someone's actions."

"Sounds like you speak from experience."

He nodded. "I was just breaking out when I met Sasha. She made me believe I was her world, but when I traveled I had trouble connecting with her. Turns out about three other guys were also her world."

"Ouch."

"Now to answer your question, it was Sasha for two years and that ended eight years ago."

I furrowed my brow. "You haven't had a relationship in eight years? I don't believe that."

"Swear to God. I mean, I've dated, but nothing lasted more than a couple of months. Often they were actresses whose schedules are just as crazy as mine. It takes a lot of work, and it's hard."

I swallowed hard. It was a harsh reminder that whatever was going on between us was just a fling. When the week was over, we would be, too.

"It's also hard for me to trust. Sasha wasn't the only one to bite me, and I'm a lot more cautious now."

"Says the man who invited a strange woman who literally ran into him in an elevator to his room, stalked her—"

He cut me off. "I did not stalk you."

I patted his forearm. "Shh, yes you did. That's my story and I'm sticking to it. You then gave her your personal phone number, like your real one, gave her your room key, chased off some bitch that works for you and rearranged your schedule to see said stranger."

"Yeah, well, you're different."

"How do you know?"

His brow scrunched. "It may be naive given my history, but I just have this feeling in my gut."

"I said it before—that's constipation."

His elbow swung out and tapped my arm. "You're this breath of fresh air. It's like my whole being lights up when I see you. Corny, I know, but that's the best way I can describe it."

"You set the butterflies off so much that I get nauseous."

"Yeah?"

There might not have been much light, but it didn't matter. I could feel the heat radiating off his skin as he leaned in. Instinctively, I turned toward it. The butterflies felt like they were going to explode from my stomach at the feel of his breath against my skin.

The soft caress of his lips against my cheek, drawing a path to my lips, left a trail of warmth. Electricity shot through me when his lips met mine. A moan left me as I wrapped my arms around his shoulders and I melted into him.

His tongue lapped against mine, and I pulled him closer.

"That's it," he said abruptly and pulled away.

I followed his lips, needing them on mine again. "Huh?"

"I know how to get out of here," he said.

CHAPTER SEVEN

I blinked at him before reaching out and pulling his face back to mine. He groaned against me, his arms wrapping around me as he tipped me down onto my back.

"Fuck," he hissed. "You are way too enticing."

"Come back," I grabbed for him as he sat back up.

"Hold on." I watched as he stood and pressed against the ceiling panels. There were sounds of metal flexing, but nothing moved.

"What are you doing?"

"Trying to get to the hatch. Elevators have an emergency hatch at the top, but you have to get past the layer of decor." He pulled at another piece and it released, popping off in his hands. "Yes!"

After laying the panel on the floor against the wall, he pulled out his phone and turned the flashlight on, shining it up and revealing the release handle.

With a hard twist, the seal popped and he pushed the lid back. It fell to the other side with a loud clang that echoed through the space. A wave of new air flowed in, making me realize how stuffy the small compartment had become.

"Come on," he said as he held out his hand.

"And go where? We should just stay."

"The power has been out for over half an hour now. We have no idea what happened or when it's coming back. Nobody knows we're here. There's a ladder against the wall. We can climb it until we reach the door and pry it open."

What he was suggesting was ludicrous. While I didn't like hanging so far up in the air, leaving was far more dangerous than staying.

"Then what? We'll be in a dark hallway," I argued as my stomach churned.

"That has access to the emergency staircase."

The switch flipped and I understood. "That unlocks automatically in a power failure."

"Exactly. We can make our way up to my room."

My excitement fell. "But there's no electricity. We can't get in," I reminded him. Everything in the hotel relied on electricity and with none, we were stuck.

"Shit, you're right."

"Then what?"

"I bust the door down, I guess."

"You sound pretty confident about all this," I said, wishing I had a fraction of his courage.

"I've done it before."

It hit me then. "A movie set is very different from real life."

"Maybe, but I'm willing to gamble. You?"

The idea alone, the danger associated with it, was fear inducing, but not as much as the idea of staying where we were.

"Maybe, especially since your idea is to climb a vertical ladder and pry an elevator door open while balancing yourself so you don't fall and leave me stranded."

"I see where your priorities lie."

"Yeah, getting my ass out of this situation intact, but I guess this is Vegas, and it's all about the gamble."

He cupped my face and tilted it back so that our eyes met. "I can do it. Trust me."

"Trust isn't the issue. One of us getting hurt is."

He pressed his lips to mine before stepping back. "We'll be okay. I promise." His fingers deftly worked open each button from his shirt, and he pulled the hem from his jeans.

"What are you doing?" I asked as I stared, transfixed at his movements.

"Too restraining. No safety nets here, and I need all the movement I can get."

That was not a comforting revelation at all. "Now you're scaring me. This is like a seriously life-threatening escape."

"Not going to lie, it's not safe, but we need to get out of here. For one thing, you seem calm, but I can tell you're suppressing the panic."

He was right. I wasn't sure how he knew, but the panic vibrated just below the surface and any opening would put me into a full on attack. "And what you're proposing will make that better?"

"When we get out, yes."

I really wished there had been lighting to watch him reach up, grab the sides, and pull himself through the opening. It was almost flawless, smooth, with only a few kicks of his legs to gain leverage. Once through he took a look around, shining the light on his phone around, then popped his head back down.

"We're at the forty-eighth floor. I can see the door for fifty." He extended his arm toward me. "Grab me, I'll pull you up."

I stuffed my phone in my back pocket and threw my purse strap over my head before clapping my hand around his wrist. He let out a strained grunt as he pulled my dead weight up until my shoulders were through the opening and I could help pull myself the rest of the way, though that didn't stop Reid from grabbing my hips and pulling them through.

The elevator shaft was even darker than the car, with only the reflective paint providing a frame of reference.

I tried not to think about the emptiness all around me, about the abyss of nothing for hundreds of feet below me, but every breath reminded me as it echoed off the concrete walls.

"I am seriously freaking out right now," I said as my teeth began to chatter. There was a difference between talking about it and sitting on top of an elevator with nothing to stop you from tumbling over the edge.

"Stop thinking about everything but the goal." He shined the light at our target about twenty-five feet up.

"How the hell are we going to get up there?"

The light swung to the right illuminating a straight vertical ladder imbedded in the wall so that it was flush.

"Hell, no." When he said ladder, I was envisioning an A frame.

"I'll go first, open the door, then you climb up and I'll help you through."

"I-I can't climb that. There's nothing...if I slip..." My chest heaved, my breaths short. He squatted down next to me.

"Shh, calm down." He caressed my cheek, his touch giving me another focus.

It was only then that I realized I'd begun to hyperventilate, my breath in panicked pants.

"Stay here. I'm going to need your help with the flashlight." I nodded, then sighed as his lips pressed against mine. "Everything is going to be okay. I'm going to get us out of here, but I need you to calm down. Can you do that for me?" I nodded. "Yes."

"Good." He pressed a kiss to the top of my head before stepping toward the ladder.

I pulled my phone out and turned on the flashlight, allowing Reid to turn his off and stuff his phone in his pocket.

I attempted to settle myself, my hands fumbling with my phone as I arranged it to point at the ladder. Reid's shoulders gave a heave as he blew out a breath, then reached out for the closest rung. My heart slammed in my chest as his hands grasped, then again as each foot settled.

He turned to me and smiled. "We're going to be fine."

If we were in a horror movie, those would be the famous last words before something tragic happened.

With each rung, my attention shifted from panic of being on top of an elevator car in a massive open shaft to staring intently as he climbed.

"Be careful," I squeaked out.

"She says once I'm ten feet up."

"Delayed reaction."

I barely took a breath until he reached the door. It was so far—how was he going to reach it? And if he did, how was he going to open it?

He answered my unasked question by shifting his position and wrapping his arm around a rung and stretched out. I hitched a breath as he reached and adjusted once again, more of his body hanging in the open.

I couldn't see much, the light only dully brightening his form. But I could hear him. Swearing and grunts as he got a grip on the door, then a guttural cry as he pulled with all his might. With a screech, a gap was created, then finally it let go, momentum helping until the door was fully open. The opening illuminated, giving to the surrounding nothingness.

Reid didn't even pause as he gripped the opening, swinging his leg over and catching the edge. He finished his climb and disappeared. A moment later his breath echoed through the chamber as he leaned over the edge from the safety of the hallway.

"Come on."

I took a few steadying breaths and climbed to my shaky legs, stuffing my phone into my back pocket. Nothing in my life had ever been as terrifying as that moment—complete blackness, nearly fifty stories beneath my unstable platform, and a vertical ladder to strength and comfort. I contemplated taking off my shoes, but decided it would probably be better to have them on.

My hands vibrated as I reached for the closest rung, Reid's phone casting enough light for me to grab hold.

With agonizing tentativeness, I placed my foot and with three points of contact, shifted my weight. A wave of calm moved through me, but it was only enough to slightly dull the terror. The solid feeling helped me to move, but it didn't necessarily make the climb any easier.

The straight up and down shifted my center of gravity, and my hands became quickly taxed by the strain.

"That's it, you're doing great," Reid cheered me on.

My muscles began to fatigue by ten feet. How had he made it look almost effortless?

Sheer will and desperation kept me going until I reached the opening. The emergency lights in the hall created a low glow while Reid kept his flashlight angled on my climb.

"Grab my hand."

It was a very different exercise than in the elevator, and much more dangerous. A slight mistake or slip could be deadly.

I reached out as far as I could while still holding onto my lifeline.

"I'm going to take your hand. When I do, hold on tight with both hands, okay?"

I nodded. "Don't let go." Fear trembled in my voice.

"I've got you. This is going to be scary, but I promise it will be okay."

His hand gripped my wrist and with one last breath, I released my other hand and stretched for his hand as gravity took over. My stomach bottomed out as I began to drop, a scream lodged in my throat. I couldn't think, couldn't process anything, but somehow as I swung up the other side of my pendulum swing, Reid used the momentum and pulled me up. My waist crashed into the opening and before I could begin to slip, there was a hard tug on my waist, hoisting me the rest of the way.

I lay on the floor, the most solid thing besides Reid's chest I'd encountered in an hour, and thanked every god I could think of.

"I'm going to be so sore in the morning," I said against the carpet.

There was a smack on my ass, Reid's fingers flexing. "Not quite the soreness I was thinking."

"Oh, Mr. Hollywood thinks I'll put out for him on the first date, huh?"

"Not really, but after getting you free from that elevator—"

"And endangering my life," I reminded him.

"And *saving* your life, maybe I might have earned some brownie points."

"I think a make-out session is ample compensation."

"I'll take it. Wait, over clothes or under?" he asked.

"Over, otherwise it becomes more."

He smacked my ass again before sitting up. "I'll still take it."

I pushed up into a sitting position and took stock of our new situation. The hallway was lit with sparse emergency lighting, just enough to help navigate to the brightly lit exit sign over what I guessed was the staircase. There was dead silence, making the already eerie situation even more so.

"Now we're in a hall, and I'm wondering if almost death was worth leaving the relative safety."

"I have to piss."

Once he said it, my bladder spoke up and agreed that not going in the confined space was probably best. Besides, the electricity was still out and worry began to creep in on if and when it would return.

"Okay, maybe you were right. And I hope all that booze is still in your room."

"Full bar," he confirmed.

"Good. I'm going to need it."

"Ditto." He took my face in his hands and our eyes met. He seemed to be studying me before his lips pressed against mine. "Are you okay?"

I nodded. "Yeah. Only slightly traumatized."

"You did great."

"Thanks."

"Are you good to go?" he asked as he stood up. He held out his hand, and I slipped mine in his as he pulled me up *again*.

"It's a good thing you're so strong."

He grinned and slipped his hand in mine. "My workouts for this film helped a ton."

The emergency stairwell didn't have much more lighting than the hallway, and the metal stairs clanged with each step. When we made it to the floor up, he tested the door and it swung open before slamming shut.

"Good sign."

We continued up, but after six floors I was tiring.

My breath was coming out in heavy pants, and my body slowed down. "Ya know, I thought I was in decent shape, but the ladder and these stairs are proving me *so* wrong."

He chuckled, his breath also heavier, but he never broke his stride.

When we finally reached the penthouse level, I fell onto the floor and sprawled out.

"Damn, it's still locked," he said, jiggling the handle.

"We thought it would be," I reminded him.

"I know, I just hoped I wasn't going to have to break down the door to my room."

"How many doors have you kicked in before?" I asked, tilting my head back to look over at him.

"Props? Many. Real ones? None."

I turned over   in time to watch him use his shoulder as a battering ram.

"Son of a bitch," he cursed, rubbing his arm.

"Are you okay?"

"Yeah." A loud bang rang out as he slammed his foot against the door, again with little movement. "Man, I make this shit look easy, and it's not."

"Bigger and thicker than you're used to."

"Stealing another of my lines."

"Oh my God!" I covered my face with my hands, not that he could really tell, and tried to ignore what he was insinuating.

Bigger and thicker made my pussy tingle in ways it hadn't in years.

He chuckled at my reaction before kicking the door again and again.

"What about the wall?" I asked as I stared at the empty space on either side of the door.

"What about it?"

"Have you ever watched *RED*?"

He paused for a second, wondering where I was going. "Yeah."

"When he had to get past a door he had no codes for?"

He stared at the space as well. "It can't be that easy."

I shrugged from my position on the floor. "You never know."

He adjusted his stance, then stopped as the emergency lights dimmed.

"I think they're running out of battery," he commented before slamming his foot into the wall next to the door.

There was a crunch, a very different sound from the bang. I sat up and crawled closer on my knees. Reid pulled out his phone and shone the light on the spot. While it wasn't a hole, it was a definite improvement from the door bashing.

"Hold this," he said as he handed his phone over.

It took a few solid kicks and some hard tugs of the firewall, but he was finally able to break through one side and then the other.

There was some metal structuring and wires, but he was able to reach through. His fingertips flicked the handle enough for me to pull the door open when the latch cleared. It was quite a stretch, half his body in the wall.

I held the door with my foot as I helped him dislodge himself, and we stepped in.

CHAPTER EIGHT

A huge relief washed over me. I'd gone through more in that evening than I thought I would in a lifetime, and I was rattled beyond belief. A sob broke through before I could stop it.

"Hey, it's okay," Reid said as he wrapped his arms around me. "You're okay."

I let the tears pour out as I shook in his arms. Almost as readily as it began, it stopped.

"I'm sorry," I said as I pulled back. "It just came out."

He ran his hands up and down my arms. "It's been a scary time, I get it. I'm going to go to the bathroom, and when I get back, I'll make us some drinks."

I nodded. "Okay."

I handed him back his phone, and he gave me a smile before walking away. With each step, the darkness surrounded me more and more until it was so dark I could only see the lighter shade of black from the windows.

It hit me then—it wasn't just the hotel.

Panic surged through me with renewed energy. I pulled out my phone and lit a path in the direction he'd headed.

"Trying to sneak up on me isn't easy in the blackout silence," he said as I entered the bathroom.

"Sorry," I said as I realized I'd just walked in on him in with his dick out. "I wasn't trying to sneak up on you."

"Everything okay?" Reid asked as he tucked himself back away.

I nodded. "Sorry, I…I'm just kinda freaked out and didn't want to be alone. The power is out everywhere."

He froze. "Everywhere?"

I nodded. "Everything is black. A giant nothingness."

He moved to the sink and flipped up the handle to wash his hands.

"I'm surprised there's water," I said as I watched, still waiting for his reaction.

"Pretty sure it's just what's in the pipes."

He dried his hands and was still a rock at the news. I couldn't decide if that made me feel better or not.

"All the way up here, I bet you're right. We had the remnants of hurricane Ike come through about ten years ago and that storm wreaked absolute havoc."

He slipped his hand in mine and we walked into the bedroom. "I remember that. I flew some friends out while their houses were worked on."

"Well, we didn't have electricity for five days, but thankfully we had water. I doubt it's the same sixty stories up."

"No, but there's probably still ice in the ice maker. What should we kick this off with?"

I thought about it. "If you've got some chips and salsa, I vote for margaritas."

"Margaritas it is."

Before heading back out, he stopped at his luggage and pulled out a large power bank. As we walked, he plugged his phone in and set it on top of the bar, screen faced down.

"That should keep us with some light for a while." The flashlight app created a pin of brightness that cast an umbrella of soft light, illuminating the room enough to navigate. However, it only worked for the immediate space.

"How long is a while?"

"Days. That thing can charge my phone ten times over."

"This better not last days," I said, my chest clenching.

"We'd be fine here. Lots of food and drinks. Blankets for warmth, and maybe that fireplace."

It was an interesting thought. What if we were stuck here for days? As I pulled off my shoes, I thought about it, and I had to admit it was intriguing. We could get to know each other very well. There would also be lots of sex. No doubt in my mind about that.

What about Sar—my thought stopped as my blood ran cold.

"Fuck," I cursed.

"We can definitely do that to keep warm," he said with a grin.

"No, Rob's plane. I hope it landed before all this." I ran up to the window and pressed my face against the glass as I attempted to look down the strip toward the airport. There was no signs of a fire from a crash anywhere, and I blew out a breath with relief.

"When was it due in?" Reid asked.

"Right around the time the power went out."

"He's fine," he assured me. "If they couldn't reach the tower they would divert to another airport, and if he landed, he's okay."

"You seem to know a lot of randomness."

He chuckled. "I've picked up a lot over the years. Plus, I do a lot of research on my roles."

"Like character research?" I asked.

"Actually, technical. Whatever the character does, I spend months learning about it. It's turned out to be a great way for me learn new and random things. It helps that I love to read."

My mind went into total and complete apocalypse scenario. Based on what I'd learned thus far, Reid would make a great survival partner. "What if the power is out everywhere?"

He paused and his head rose, his eyes meeting mine. "I think it's just Vegas."

"Why do you think that?" I asked. Did he know something, or was it just a silent prayer?

"Not a thought, but a hope." He stepped up next to me and stared out. "Fuck."

There was only a few small bright spots, like the twinkling of stars around. Not enough to illuminate much, but enough to be a beacon of life.

"I've never been anywhere so dark. There's hardly any moon. And the stars—I've never seen the Milky Way so clearly." There was a streak of what looked like clouds and light that was millions of stars. They were the only light in the dark sky.

Reid's hand slipped into mine, our fingers intertwining.

"It's okay if you're not okay," I whispered.

He didn't respond, but kissed my forehead before stepping back to the bar.

"Are we really going to spend all night in your room?" I asked as I continued to stare out into the blackness. It was almost like the glass wasn't there—black upon black.

"Do you have a better idea? We're safe up here."

"It's not that. I'm just wondering what's going on down there." In the distance, I saw a fire that wasn't a bonfire, possibly a building.

The rumble of ice against glass was all I could hear as he filled up two glasses. "What do you mean?"

"Think about it—thousands of people, no electricity."

"Societal breakdown?" he asked.

"Maybe. Or is everyone sitting in the lobby getting drunk in the dark."

"That's probably not a good combination."

"No, but I have a feeling it's mass chaos in the streets. Do they have some kind of protocol in place for this?" I wondered.

"I doubt it. That's the whole purpose of the backup generators. And with no communications…"

I didn't want to think too hard on what it was like down there. If I hadn't been with Reid, what would I have done? Where would I have gone?

"I'm suddenly really glad you forgot your wallet and that I came up with you. I'd be freaking out down there by myself."

"If you hadn't come with me, I would have gotten out of the elevator sooner and gone to find you."

My heart sped up for a second as I stared at him. "Really? You would've come to find me?"

"I can't be the hero if you're not there to see it," he said, that playful smirk gracing his face.

"Oh, that's how it is," I said as I walked back over to him. "All for the glory."

"Not glory so much as wanting to impress you."

I froze. Of all the men I'd met before, not one would have done anything close to what Reid had done. In fact, I wasn't sure any of them would have given half the effort Reid had in the last few days. "You're impressive enough as it is."

He strode toward me carrying our drinks, but it was too dark to see his expression as he handed me a glass. "Toast?"

"Bread."

"What?" He let out a chuckle. "Random much?"

I shook my head. "Sorry, my brother and I always used to play stupid word games like that."

"Do I remind you of your brother?" he asked.

"Not at all," I quickly answered. "That would be gross if I thought about him the way I think about you."

"How do you think about me?"

I held my glass up. "You're one of a kind, Reid Gallagher, and I'm so unbelievably lucky to have met you and gotten to spend time with you. You scare me, but at the same time, you make me feel like I could fly. So, a toast, to whatever this warmth is that spreads through me when I'm near you."

"To wherever this takes us."

We clinked our glasses, and I took a sip of my margarita. "Mmm," I said in surprise. "Wow, that's good."

"Thanks." He set his down on the coffee table before going back and retrieving the only source of light and our snacks.

"Got any other hidden talents?" I asked before taking another sip.

I could see his grin as he walked over. It looked a little maniacal thanks to the harsh shadows. "Many. If you're a good girl, maybe I'll show you later."

"What do bad girls get?"

He let out a groan as he sat. "What happened to PG?"

"Darkness? Adrenaline? Near death experience? Being within a ten-foot radius of you?"

"Let's go back to twenty questions," he said as he held out a chip loaded with salsa.

"Really?" I asked as I bit down on the chip, my hand cupping underneath to catch any of the bits that were threatening to escape.

"Need to cool things down."

"Are you sure?" I asked. "Sorry. I just, this whole night..." I looked down to my glass. "You really are my savior, Reid."

He brushed my hair back and tilted my chin up. "Don't be sorry. It's just that I don't—" He blew out a breath. "I have a strong draw to you, and I want you, very much, but I don't want it to all be physical."

"I'm sorry."

"Stop being sorry. Now, back to twenty questions. How long have you been friends with Sarah?"

He shoveled another chip into his mouth, then held one out for me.

"Having you feed me is kinda fun," I said as I took the bite.

"Then I'm doing this right."

"Doing what right?" I asked.

He leaned in closer. "Wooing you."

I ducked my head and took another sip of my drink. Fuck. He needed to stop being so charming, or I was going to be in serious trouble. "We were college roommates. Met as fresh-faced freshmen and we clicked."

"Like you and me?" he asked. Again, charmer needed to stop charming because he was making me a melty mess of emotions.

Another chip sat at my lips, and I leaned forward and chomped on it. "Well, *we* click on a level I've never clicked on with her."

He let out a deep chuckle. "Good to know where my competition lies."

"You think there's competition? Ha!"

"There's always some sort of competition."

"What's mine?" I asked.

He reached up and caressed my cheek, the smile gone from his face. "Time."

I froze, expecting him to say something about all the beauties who surrounded him daily.

He let out a sigh. "Free time is something I don't have a lot of, but I would give it all to you. Maybe not in person, but any way I could."

"You would give it all to me?"

He caressed my cheek, his eyes locked on mine. "I will."

My gaze jumped between his eyes looking for some sort of humor or deception, but I found neither. Instead, I found what I could only describe as longing.

"Did you get into acting for the fame?" I asked, changing the subject away from the ones that made my stomach do somersaults.

"I want to say no, but I think that's more of a hindsight revelation. In the beginning, getting recognized on the street for my face on the screen was amazing and such a rush, but it changes you—and not in the way most expect."

"Really? How did it change you?" I asked.

"You saw how Kimber was. Well, she's that way with good reason."

"The whole *you don't make friends that fast* attitude?" I tipped my glass back to suck down the last bits of salty lime-ness.

"Exactly. There's a serious lack of privacy, cameras always in your face wherever you go. People want to use you for how you can help them, or what the status being in your circle can do for them." He stood and took my glass and the light. I watched the glow move away over to the bar as he refreshed our drinks. "Even Kimber has been used to get to me. It was a hard lesson for her and a restraining order for me. You become rude to people when you don't want to be, simply because being nice invites them to take advantage of you."

"Wow," was all I could say. "All of that is a high price."

"It is, and I don't want to knock it, because I love what I do, so that's why I treasure time with the people I trust. There's no pretense or nefarious goal."

"Well, the only nefarious goal I have is getting to know you better," I said as I watched him expertly pour the tequila.

"That's not nefarious. I think you need a dictionary recap."

"Well, it may not be, but it's my only goal. Besides taking advantage of you in the bedroom."

"Bedroom?" He cocked a brow at me.

"Or couch, table, floor." I gestured around the room. "Really anywhere."

He let out another groan as he walked back over and handed me my refilled glass. "Where do you see yourself in ten years?"

"Is this an interview?" I asked as I took another hit of the strong liquid.

His shoulders gave a shrug as he sat. "In a way."

What did I want? Over the last few months the only thing I wanted was to not feel so miserable and used. I wanted the opposite of that. "In ten years I see myself happy. I hope."

"What does happy mean to you?" he asked before taking a long pull.

Happy. Happy.

There was only one image that came to mind.

"In love, married, children. Sharing my life with a man I love. A deep love, where there is no doubt he loves me. What about you?"

"Oddly, pretty much the same, only change man to woman."

Envisioning Reid holding a baby was ovary explosion inducing. A sexy daddy that could take care of his baby on his own, as well as take care of his wife.

The next image that popped up was him with some super thin model or actress with perfect hair and makeup and very opposite of me.

"Margaritas also make me happy," I said in an attempt to wipe the thoughts from my mind.

"Do they?" he asked, a seductive edge to his tone.

"And you make good ones."

He leaned in closer. "Does that make me a keeper?"

"Are you asking if you're ten-year material?"

"Maybe."

My heart began to slam wildly in my chest. "Maybe you are."

"Maybe I could be."

Reid made strong margaritas, and by the time I finished the second one, I was straddling his lap, his hands lazily trailing up and down my sides. I'd reached that happy, horny state. Pleasantly buzzed, but not drunk. My inhibitions were lowered, and I relaxed a bit.

"I think you got me tipsy on purpose," I said as I pulled his glass to my lips.

He fed me another chip with salsa on it in an attempt to soak up the drinks. "Not on purpose, but I will admit I was curious about tipsy Harper." His hands continued their path up and down my sides. Much like the magnet he talked about being, I was drawn closer, my chest pressed against his, my lips inches from his.

I reached between us and cupped his length. "You don't need to get me drunk to have sex with you."

He let out a groan, his hands settling on my hips. "I know. You told me." He leaned forward and nipped at my neck before kissing and sucking his way up and then back down. "Fuck, Harper." He took hold of my hand and pulled it from his warm length, placing it on his chest as he leaned back. "You're making it fucking hard for me to be a gentleman."

"Making it hard is kinda the point. And who said I wanted a gentleman?"

"What do you want?"

"A beast. A brute who takes what he wants from my body." I leaned back, one hand on his shoulder, the other in my hair as I rotated my hips. "I want to feel desperation, desire." My lips touched his lightly as our eyes locked. "I want you to want me like you've never wanted anyone before."

His fingers dug into my hips, holding me close. "When was the last time a man gave you an orgasm?"

A gasp left me, and my hips gave an involuntary rotation. "Never. When was the last time you gave a woman an orgasm?"

His hands ran up and around my neck, fingers threading through my hair as he pulled me closer, his lips ghosting mine. "Ask me in an hour."

CHAPTER NINE

His hands were harsh, full of that need I so desperately craved. His mouth attacked my skin like a starving man.

"Harper," he hissed. He nipped his way up to my lips, kissing me with a fervor that engulfed me. Set every inch of me on fire—a combustible flame only he could extinguish.

A moan left me as his hands squeezed at my breasts, his fingers pinching my nipples through the thin fabric of my top. He was the sweetest torture. I needed more, wanted him to fuck me raw, but Reid was in control and I loved every second of it.

His attempts to get his hands against my skin were thwarted by the design of the bodysuit, and a low growl left him. His fingers trailed against the exposed skin of the keyhole cutout, slipping under as he hastily searched for a way to get it off.

"What the fuck is this?"

"A bodysuit." I reached behind me to unclasp the buttons at the back of my neck when I heard him growl.

"Fuck this." With a strong tug he pulled at the fabric, the center seam giving way. He continued until the line of exposed skin slipped below the waistband of my jeans. The tug forced the fabric against my clit and my nails dug into his arms.

"Oh, God," I moaned, eyes closing as a low keening sound left me.

I wanted him. Something he knew.

"You look so good being needy. Wanting my cock." His lips closed around a pebbled nipple, flicking the sensitive skin with his tongue before pulling back to blow.

A gasp left me as cool air hit my skin, my nipples pebbling. Every touch fueled the fire that raged through my body. My skin buzzed with the electricity that sparked between us.

"Please." I took hold of his belt, my hips undulating, seeking any friction.

"Stay still," he hissed. One of his hands took hold of mine and pinned them behind my back, holding me still. I was at his mercy, bound and unable to move.

I fucking loved it.

"Please, Reid. I need more."

"Fuck, I love the way you say my name. So pretty."

"Let me touch you," I whimpered. "I want to feel you." My hips moved against his length, pushing down while his mouth continued his assault on my chest.

He pulled back, and even in the dim light I could see how hooded his eyes were. Reaching up, he threaded his hand into my hair and pulled me to him, our lips crashing.

I needed to feel his skin, was desperate to. Clawing at his shirt, I yanked it over his head, uncaring if it survived. The peek I'd gotten of his chest the other day was just a warm up for the main attraction.

"Christ," I said in awe as I ran my hands around his abs, fingers dipping into each indentation. And then lower.

Deftly I worked open his belt, then the button and zipper. I slipped my hand beneath his waistband, fingers grazing his hard shaft. There was a hitch in his breath as I trailed up to the head, my finger swirling around a bead of pre-come there before bringing the glistening digit to my lips.

His taste was heady. All man and addictive.

"Motherfuck," he bit out. His fingers dug into my hips as his own flexed up.

He fisted my hair and tipped me backwards, practically throwing me down on the coffee table. I let out a squeak, but barely had time to process it when he popped the button of my jeans and pulled them down my legs, leaving me in only my torn bodysuit.

I peered at him while he stared at my body. With one hand, he palmed a breast while the other trailed down the torn seam. When he reached the end he pulled, making me gasp and causing my back to arch, the seam brushing my clit again. A low growl left him before he did in again, making me writhe against the table.

"Fuck," I whimpered.

Both of his hands gripped the fabric and continued its decimation. The sound of ripping cloth filled the silent air, and my body was pulled and twisted until the bodysuit was a pile of scrap on the floor.

He settled between my open thighs, his hands trailing down to my knees before pinning them against the table. The feel of his hot cockhead pressed against my clit had me bucking against his grip, desperate to feel more of him. Every nerve begged for it, to feel him fill me, to give me the pleasure I'd been denied.

Pleasure only he could give.

"Tell me what you want."

I reached between us and wrapped my hand around his shaft, loving the feel of how hot and hard he was. "I want you inside me. I want you to fuck me."

He slipped from my grip and his head dove between my legs, tongue swiping up my slit before giving my clit a flick. I squirmed from the sudden intensity but could only whimper and grip the edge of the table as his arms held my thighs tight, leaving only my hips to buck against his face.

Nobody had eaten me out in years, probably since college, and my mind couldn't handle the pleasure that rang through me.

"Reid! Oh God, please. Please, Reid," I cried, my eyes rolling back as my muscles tightened, but he didn't let up, only licked and rubbed harder. His fingers joined in, fucking me, getting me ready for him.

Every breath was stunted, half of it sacrificed to the pleasure that was quickly driving me insane. I couldn't think, only feel and only at his pace. My shoulders and head were all that touched the table, my body bent for him to devour and for me to see. His eyes met mine and my mouth dropped open, muscles coiled tight.

The edge was close, so close, and so strong I was almost afraid, but there was nothing I could do. My vision became unfocused and my back arched as I failed to draw in a breath.

And then snap.

A scream left me, my hips rocking against his face as I jerked against him, my pussy pulsing as I shook. He backed off and slowed, kissing down my thigh as he lowered me back to the table. Strength left me as I tried to regain my breath.

"Ask me."

"How long since you gave an orgasm?" I said between stunted pants.

He beamed down at me, obviously proud of himself. "Thirty seconds, give or take." He reached out and ran his hands up my thighs, thumbs skimming my outer lips on their way up to grab my breasts. "You're so delicious I could do that every day."

"Okay. Go for it."

He chuckled, his touch deepening. While I may have come, he had not, and the way he moved around my body left my skin burning even more. It was that touch I'd craved for so long, the one that sat deep in my bones in an unfulfilling relationship.

After a minute of recovery, he stood and moved over near my head. I salivated at the sight of his cock still protruding from his jeans, my pussy clenching. It was long and thick and so hard as it pointed at me.

He pushed his pants down, making sure he was free of the cloth.

"Wet it." His tone was deep and commanding, and I wanted to give him everything he asked for.

I craned my neck up and flicked the tip before closing my lips around the head. A deep moan left him, and I reached out to grab his thighs to bring him closer as I slowly worked my way down his shaft, then back up.

I loved a vocal man, and Reid made certain I knew how good it felt simply by the sounds he made.

He stepped back, his chest heaving, and pulled something from his pocket as he shed his jeans. I'd been on birth control for years, but Jeremy still wore a condom every time.

All I wanted was to feel Reid. Every inch of him.

"I'm clean," I said as my hand slipped between my thighs to rub against my clit. "Tested two months ago, and I haven't had sex in over eight."

He froze and stared at me, his gaze trapped to where my hand was. "Same."

"Same?" I needed clarification before I asked him.

"Tested six months ago, haven't in ten."

"How did I say I wanted it?" I asked, pushing him in the direction I was desperate for.

"Fuck," he cursed, his jaw locked tight. I could tell he was restraining himself, warring with his desire.

A gasp left me, my fingers pinching my clit. "Take me. Bare."

Even in the dim light his expression said so much, and the condom was forgotten on the floor. In a second he was between my legs again, positioned, and stretching me in one thrust.

I drew in a breath as he slammed forward. Each inch made my back arch more and more, and my eyes to roll back. A couple rotations of his hips and he was completely buried.

Every nerve lit up again, heat and pleasure spiking through my blood. With one hand fisted in my hair and the other pinning my hip to the table, he set up a brutal pace. Each time he bottomed out, I let out a loud keening sound. With all the foreplay, it didn't take long for his strokes to falter.

"Fuck," he groaned as he pulled out, grunting as he fisted his cock, firing off. Rope after rope of warm cum landed on my stomach, some reaching my breasts.

Once done, he fell back to the floor on his haunches, his arms draped over my legs. He took a minute to catch his breath, his eyes never leaving mine.

With the scrap of my former top, he wiped away the rapidly cooling cum from my skin. "Fuck."

"What?" I asked as I propped myself up on my elbows.

"You're the girl who came from my dreams, but you also crawled out of every fantasy I've ever had."

Reaching up, I caressed his cheek and drew him down, our lips meeting in a searing kiss. "Yeah, I'm going to have to go with ditto there."

He beamed down at me before grabbing our only light and sweeping his arms under my body, picking me up from the table and carrying me bridal style.

"Where are we going?" I asked as I took the opportunity to kiss and nip at his neck.

"Do you feel thoroughly taken?"

A contented sigh left me. I was already limp in his arms. "Yes."

"Good. Now I'm going to fuck you slow, hard, and deep. Make this pussy never want another cock but mine."

I didn't have the strength to tell him he'd already accomplished his goal. Besides, I was looking forward to him working me hard again.

CHAPTER TEN

Beeping. Little blips rang in my ears, stirring me from my fantastic dream. When my pillow moved, my brain kicked in and I remembered where I was and who I was with.

I slipped from his chest as he reached over to the nightstand.

"Your phone is going ballistic."

"Yeah…" he trailed off as he rolled back over. "Guess the power is finally back on." He scanned the messages that were still beeping in. "Everyone is checking in. News spread, it seems. Nothing major. Though they've already pushed off today's schedule until they can account for everyone."

"Does that mean we get to stay in bed?" I asked with a kiss against his shoulder, and then a nip because the man was simply delicious.

His lips curled into a smirk. "I thought you'd never ask."

Just then my phone went off and I reached across him, pulling the cord to the power bank out. Sarah's name was on the screen, and I quickly answered as I sat up.

"Sarah? Oh my God! Are you okay? Is Rob with you?"

"We're okay. The power went out when they started unloading the plane. Long night at the airport and it was mass chaos, but we're okay." By all the chatter in the background, I could only imagine what it was like. "We're working on getting back to the hotel."

"Thank God. I've been so worried."

"Where were you?" she asked, moving a little away from all the noise.

My gaze shifted to his, and I felt my face heat up. "Reid and I were in the elevator when it went out."

"Oh shit. Are you okay?" she asked.

"I'm fine. Reid made sure of it." Reid's head popped up from his phone and he turned onto his side, that sexy smirk growing on his gorgeous face as his hand crawled up my blanket-covered leg. "I'll tell you all about it later, but it turned out to be a real-life action movie experience and now we're safe in his room."

"I can't wait to hear all the juicy details." The emphasis on juicy meant her best-friend-spidey-senses were working. "Not sure when we'll be back, but we're both in desperate need of a shower and bed, so we might not be sociable until dinner."

It was hard to hold in the moan that wanted to crawl out from Reid's hand gripping my thigh. "That's okay. I think I can find some way to keep myself busy."

"I bet. We'll see you soon."

"Be safe."

I hung up the phone and barely had it set down before Reid attacked. His hands took hold of my hips and tugged, pinning me beneath him, drawing me to him.

"Hi." I giggled, looking up at him.

He dipped down and nipped my bottom lip. "Hi. Guess my question of *what are you doing for breakfast* is answered."

"Oh, yeah? Are you the answer?"

"Well, I was going to suggest room service if they're going, but now that you mention it..." His hand trailed down my side, then lower, dipping beneath me to take hold of my ass. "You are quite tasty."

Just then my stomach gave a grumble, and we both broke out into laughter. "Guess we should see if breakfast is a possibility. And if room service isn't available, there has got to be something in that kitchen, right?"

He gave a shrug. "I'm not sure."

I wondered if this man could ever look any other way than sexy as fuck. Naked chest, disheveled hair, and that little smirk that always seemed to be present.

Pushing him back, I sat up, straddled his hips, and grabbed my phone again. "Give me a sec."

"What are you doing?" he asked as I held my phone in front of me, aiming the camera at him.

"Evidence this wasn't all a dream." I snapped half a dozen quick shots before he tugged me back down into the crook of his arm. He took the phone from me and rotated the camera, holding it high.

"Say cheese."

"Oh, God. I look terrible!" Turning my face into his chest, I attempted to hide how horrible I looked.

"You look beautiful," he said, placing a kiss to my forehead and taking another picture.

When he was done, he sent a few to himself before grabbing his phone and getting a few more shots of us, then rolled me onto my back once more and straddled my waist.

"Wait!" I cried out as I shielded my breasts. He grabbed one and squeezed it for a few more camera snaps. "Is that considered helping?"

"It's keeping my dick hard as fuck."

It sure was. I glanced down and watched the tip bounce and tap my stomach. My thighs clenched at the sight, loving my first look of it in the light. Was there any part of him that wasn't perfect?

"Well I know you don't have any issues with that."

He grinned down at me and removed his hand, only to slip it between my thighs. A gasp left me as his fingers rubbed at my clit. With him straddling me I couldn't roll away, could only arch my back and buck my hips against him.

"Reid," I whimpered as I bit down on the top of my finger.

"Mmm, I like having you at my mercy like this."

He slipped a digit inside, and I threw my head back and moaned. I was sore from the night before, but that didn't seem to matter when he touched me. My whole body lit up again, pleasure zipping through my veins. I grabbed hold of his thighs for some sort of leverage against him, but that only caused him to speed up his fingering and add another as he drove deeper.

I really was completely at his mercy.

His hand left me, but I didn't have any time to recover before his weight moved from on top of me to beside me. I was swept up with one arm while the other returned. A growl left him before his mouth latched onto my breast, tongue flicking my sensitive nipple and sending shocks down to my clit.

My mind had gone fuzzy, completely focused on what he was doing, building to my impending orgasm. He gripped me tighter as my muscles coiled, back arching, and he never slowed down.

Everything froze, then snapped, and a scream left me as I began shuddering in his arms. His mouth moved up my chest, kissing and nipping until he reached my mouth.

"Fuck, you're beautiful," he said as he slowed, then positioned himself between my thighs, one of my legs pinned to the mattress. I was still coming down when he pressed forward, stretching me open.

My pussy clenched and pulsed around him. Low groans rumbled deep in his chest, hips flexing in long, deep strokes.

"So good," he groaned before he sped up.

Even with my mind a fog, I agreed with him. He felt so good.

His lips were close to my ear, letting me hear every moan, every little bit of pleasure. "I want to come in you."

Fire zipped from where we were joined to the top of my head. "Yes." I wanted him to as well. I needed to feel it.

A few more hard thrusts and his hips slammed into mine, a roar leaving him as his cock exploded inside me. I clenched around him, my nails digging into his back, legs fastened around his waist, holding him close as I got lost with him.

With the last jerk he collapsed down, holding his weight up by his forearms so not to crush me, but still buried deep inside me.

"Wow," I said, my arms going lax and sliding down beside me.

"Wow is right." He was breathing hard, trying to catch his breath. "You need to stop turning me on before you drain me dry."

I arched a brow at him, silently loving that I seemed to have so much sway over him. "You're the one incapable of keeping your hands to yourself."

He smirked down at me. "You're the one that keeps flashing me your boobs. I'm a breast man. You can't do that if you can't handle the consequences." We broke out into laughter, his forehead falling to mine. "Come on, let's go get cleaned up." He pulled me close and picked me up before walking us to the bathroom. Something about a man being able to carry me anywhere was such a turn-on.

There was a low rumble in his chest as he stood in the middle of the room. "Now that's a great view."

I craned my head around to see our reflection and the way his fingers dug into my cheeks, spreading them, presenting a view of his cock stretching me. Slowly he pulled me up until he slipped from inside me. He continued to stare transfixed at the mirror, watching the pearly white droplets fall from my pussy to the tile beneath.

After reluctantly putting me down on the ground and steadying me, Reid spun to turn the water on and my eyes popped wide.

Long red and pink marks marred his skin. They covered his shoulders, the back of his biceps, and even his ass.

"Holy shit."

"What?" At my wide-eyed stare, he moved back to the mirror and stretched to get a look. "Holy shit is right. Damn, baby. Guess I did a good job. At least that explains the stinging."

I shook my head. "I didn't do that. Nope."

"Nobody else was here, and I sure as hell didn't have them when I picked you up last night." He had that playful smile on his lips as he took my hand and held it up against one of the marks. The spacing was same.

"I-I've never done anything like that before," I said, still in shock that I was the one responsible.

"Deena in makeup is going to have a field day with this."

"Oh my God!" I slapped his arm. "Don't say that." Heat flooded my face as mortification set in, and I hid my face with my hands. I hadn't even thought about the fact that it wasn't just the two of us that would see the marks.

"Hey, hey." He pulled my hands away and moved them to wrap around his waist. "Don't worry about it, I want the world to see your mark on me," he said, pressing his lips to mine. "Now I just have to figure out how to mark you."

"Seeing as I've been covered in your cum, I think you've accomplished that."

"I did come in you," he reminded me, a smirk playing on his lips.

My eyes widened. "We're you trying to knock me up?"

He shook his head. "No, I promise. It's just the thought of fucking a baby into you is sexy as fuck."

I'd never thought about it before, but the way he said it made me want it, too. "I'm on birth control anyway."

"Hmm, are hickies still a thing?" he asked, still trying to find a way to mark me.

"Maybe for high school kids. Though, you did mention something about biting…" I trailed off and shyly smiled at him.

He licked his lips as he smirked at me. "I did." He lifted me off my feet and walked me into the shower. "Let's see what we can do about that."

After a shower, and Reid's attempts to mark me, we found that room service wasn't up and running yet, so we decided to see what the kitchen held.

"I'm borrowing a shirt," I said as I picked a T-shirt up from his suitcase. There was a bit of a chill in the air, and he'd destroyed my top the night before. I also grabbed a pair of sweatpants for now, rolling the waist multiple times to keep them from falling down.

"I hope that means I'll have the opportunity to get it back."

"You could get it back on Saturday," I said, wishing I hadn't as soon as the words were out. There was no way he would want to or even be able to go to Sarah's wedding.

"What's Saturday?"

"Would you...I mean..." I blew out a breath and fidgeted with the hem of the shirt. "Would you want to come to Sarah's wedding as my date?"

He tapped his fingers against my hip. "That depends."

"On?"

"If I can have you for every minute after that."

My heart skipped and I relaxed, leaning into him. "Until I leave."

"I was thinking a bit longer than that."

"Longer?" I questioned in confusion, looking up at him.

"I'd love for you to stay longer," he admitted. "I don't know what this is, what's going on, but I can't just watch you walk away. Not yet."

I shook my head. "This is crazy."

"I know."

"We just met."

"So, here's my number."

"Call me maybe?"

His fingers trailed across my cheek. "No, no maybe. Definitely. I don't know what it is, but I have this weird feeling. A good weird, and I want to see where it goes."

After breakfast, we were fueled, giving Reid the energy to strip me down and go again. The man was a machine, and I happily reaped all the benefits.

It was mid-afternoon when his phone went off and he let out a groan—they were going to be ready for makeup in an hour.

It worked out well, timing wise, or else I might not have been able to pry myself from him to meet Sarah and Rob for dinner.

"I hate to leave," I said, slipping my jeans on.

"Then don't." He sat on the edge of the bed, pulling his socks on.

"I've had a great time, handsome. Even with all the near-death experiences." I leaned down and pressed my lips to his, taking a bit of his scent and taste with me. "But you've been called in, and I need to get ready for dinner."

"It was fun, despite the craziness," he said with a wink.

"I wouldn't have wanted to have it with anyone else," I admitted, and it was the truth. Saying it out loud stung a bit because the connection was real. We clicked. We felt right together.

He leaned forward for another kiss. "Same. I'm serious, I want to see you again."

"Really?"

"Are you going to make me go all stalker on you again?" His smirk made me want to nip his bottom lip, then soothe it with my tongue, but that would start something we didn't have time to finish.

"That was kinda fun."

"Fun?" He quirked a brow.

Shrugging, I smiled. "I like you chasing me."

"Then I'll chase you until I can catch you."

Could he be real, or just telling me what I wanted to hear? Hope fluttered in my chest and made me want the impossible.

More him.

More us.

"But what happens when the week is over?"

"We keep it going, just from a distance." Reid made it all sound so simple. He had his life, and I had mine. Our worlds didn't mix, and we weren't a Hollywood romance—the world he lived in and dominated.

"Our lives are so different." My tone was flat, the realist in me surfacing.

"Just because it's hard doesn't mean it's not worth trying."

"You're very pushy about this."

He stood and slipped his finger in my belt loop, pulling me until my hands rested on his chest. "There's a reason why."

"And what's that?" I needed to understand why. A reason to keep the tiny bit of hope alive in my chest.

"I've never met anyone who affects me like you do, and I want to know more. I'm not ready to just toss this aside as a good time."

"Isn't that what you do?" I slapped my hand over my mouth, but the words were out before I could stop them.

"Ouch."

"I'm sorry," I whispered low, a lump caught in my throat. He'd never given me any indication of being anything other than strong and sweet and sincere. "My insecurities are rearing their ugly heads. Please, forgive that."

He lifted my chin, forcing my eyes to meet his. "It was a genuine expression of your feelings, even if they are misplaced."

"It's just…I leave here and this wonderful dream ends."

He brushed a strand of hair from my face and cupped my cheek. "It's not the end. This is just the beginning." He pressed his lips to mine for a searing kiss. "Later, beautiful. That's a promise."

One last kiss, one last hug, and I reluctantly made my way out to the elevator.

"I'll see you Saturday, and every day leading up to it," he said, his hand slipping into mine.

"Saturday."

The elevator arrived, and I stepped on for it to take me away from the most exciting time of my life. I blew him a kiss, and cherished every last second before the doors blocked the view.

I wasn't sure what our future held, but I was going to enjoy the time we had.

CHAPTER ELEVEN

It took a while for Vegas to recoup from the blackout. While the authorities were still investigating what happened, order was restored, and by midday Thursday, things were almost back to normal.

Stay with me tonight – Reid

I smiled down at my phone. He'd been filming since I left him the day before, but he still managed to contact me. I had a slew of text messages and photos from him.

"Wow, now that's a happy smile," Sarah said as she sat next to me. "What did Mr. Hollywood say now?"

"He wants me to stay with him tonight."

"If you haven't typed back a yes yet, hand over the phone and I'll do it for you."

I rolled my eyes. "I'm perfectly capable of doing it myself."

What was supposed to be a return around six turned out to be ten, and he was wiped. A quick shower, then he threw me onto the bed, wrapped his arms around me, and fell asleep.

When I awoke with the sun on Friday, he was gone.

Morning, beautiful. Didn't want to wake you. I'll call you later – Reid

The day was spent in the casino, more and more of the wedding party arriving every hour. The more people who arrived, the less of Sarah I had, but thankfully I had Reid to keep me company, even if it was through the phone. Nearly every hour I got a run-by kiss or text message, but barely a minute of his time.

"You're still good to come, right?" I asked him on the phone as I stood outside the restaurant hosting the rehearsal dinner.

"Got my suit all out and ready," he said.

"Good."

"Only wish I could see you tonight," I said. I missed him, very much.

"I'll see you tomorrow."

"I miss you."

My heart clenched. "I miss you, too."

Sarah stayed with me that night to keep up with the tradition of being separate from the groom. The next day was joyous and full of smiles. I'd never seen Sarah happier. She was so beautiful in her dress. The smile on Rob's face couldn't be contained as he watched her walk down the aisle to him.

The ceremony was beautiful. I'd never seen Sarah happier or with a bigger smile. Rob's gaze was glued to her from the second he saw her, and it never left. Soon after, the festivities began and I still hadn't heard from Reid, but I tried not to let it get me down.

My phone went off, and my heart skipped at Reid's name on the screen.

"Hi! Where are you?" I asked, hoping he was close.

"Harper, I'm sorry," he said. I could hear it in his voice— remorse.

I sat down, the light draining from me. "You're not coming, are you?"

"I just got a call. They need me on set."

"But you had tonight off," I said, a whining edge to my voice.

"It happens. Things shift and move. I'm so sorry. I really wanted to go."

Tears began to well in my eyes. "I understand." And I did. I just didn't like it.

"What time is your flight tomorrow?" he asked.

"Noon."

"Maybe we can have breakfast?"

"Maybe." There was no way I could hide the disappointment in my voice. I had undiluted access to him for almost twenty-four hours, but as soon as things resumed on regular schedule, nothing worked out.

"Have fun tonight. I was really looking forward to dancing with you, kissing you, being with you."

"Me, too," I sniffed. In the background, I heard a bunch of commotion, followed by his name being called over what sounded like a bullhorn.

He sighed. "I've got to go. Have a good night. Send me a pic."

"Okay. Good luck."

I swiped a tear away as I hung up. It hadn't even been a week since we met, but it felt like so much longer. The depth of my emotions for him were so much more than I could ever have anticipated when I'd first bumped into him.

He'd been dead on when he said my competition was time, because there never seemed to be any for me.

I was so happy for my best friend, but inside I was a mess. Inside was an immense sadness I couldn't even fathom.

"This is my day," Sarah said, standing in front of my with her hands on her hips. "I'm the bride. You're supposed to be happy and excited and joyous."

"I'm sorry." And I was. I wanted to be all those things, but my heart was somewhere else.

She sat down next to me and threw her arm over my shoulders. "I know I pushed for it, for you to go out with him. I just didn't expect for you to fall for him so hard."

I blew out a breath. "Neither did I."

"Maybe him not coming is a good thing."

"Good how?"

"The last few days, you've seen just how busy he is and how unexpectedly it can change. It gives you a realistic view of his life," she said, her head tilting to rest on mine.

"I knew from the beginning it would never work past Vegas, but a part of me hoped." That girlish hope for a fantasy I knew couldn't be a reality. "The part of me that allowed myself to feel so much for him in such a short time."

"At least now you know you can have feelings like that again," she pointed out. "Jeremy didn't take that from you. So, you had a rebound with one of the hottest actors ever. It gets you back out there."

I shook my head, my brow furrowed. "The thing is, Reid isn't a rebound."

He was so very much more.

***

Good morning, beautiful. How was the wedding? – Reid

Are you still in the hotel? – Reid

Where are you? I just went to your room – Reid

Harper, please – Reid

Don't leave until I see you – Reid

I stared down at the slew of text messages, each one breaking my heart further. Every ping I heard, every call ignored, but when I finally looked at the texts, there was no stopping the tears from flowing.

It was like a breakup, a true breakup and not just the end to a beautiful time together. The hit was harder to my system than Jeremy telling me I was nothing but a placeholder.

I'd gone down to the lobby to pick up a few souvenirs at the gift shop, including a deck of the casino's playing cards. All that was left was to finish zipping up my bags and check out before heading to the airport.

"Harper!" I heard my name called out in Reid's familiar voice. I tried to ignore it, tried to will the elevator doors open so I could jump in and blot out the sound of my name coming from his perfect lips.

A zing zipped up my arm, causing me to draw in a sharp breath as Reid touched me. I turned to him, but didn't get to look at him before his arms were around me and my head was against his chest.

"Why are you ignoring me?"

My fingers fisted around the fabric of his shirt. It was hard to believe that the most wonderful week of my life was over, and it hurt worse than I could ever have imagined. "I have to get to the airport."

"I know. I just." He heaved a sigh. "I wanted to see you before you go."

My chest clenched. It was the hard part after a dream-like encounter. Reluctantly I pulled away, stepping back. "That's probably not a good idea."

He was silent. "Why?"

"You know why," I whispered. I couldn't even look at him because my chest was ripping open.

"So this is it?" he asked.

"Yes."

"I can't believe you're just giving up."

I snap my head up to look at him. "It's not easy, Reid."

His eyes were filled with hurt and anger. "It sure sounds easy."

"Well, it's not. But I'm a realist, and the last two days have opened my eyes from this fairy tale. We live thousands of miles apart. How is that going to work?"

"You're not even willing to try?" he asked, his brow furrowed. "You're just fucking giving up?"

"If I don't do it now, it's going to hurt so much worse later. I like you. Far more than I should," I admitted. If I didn't do it now, I never would.

"I like you, too, and I'm not ready to throw in the towel."

Silence stretched between us. My heart wanted to agree, but my head refused to let it. The pain I felt was already so great.

"I've got to get to the airport," I said as I started to pull away.

"Let's talk. Please. Let's go to your room and talk. Just give me five minutes."

I shook my head. "It's not going to change anything. Thank you for a great week." The doors slid open, and I took my first steps away from him.

"Harper!" He reached out and grabbed my hand, stopping me.

"Let me go," I said, barely able to contain the sob building in my chest.

"Don't I get a say in this?" he asked.

I drew in a ragged breath and turned to him. His expression was begging, pleading, and I was unable to hold back a small sob, the tears filling my eyes falling to my cheeks.

"I really wish you nothing but the best, Reid. Goodbye."

As soon as the elevator doors closed, I let loose the sob I'd been holding onto, not caring about the other people in the car.

When I returned to my room, I took a few minutes to settle myself before packing up the last few items and leaving. I checked out, and I grabbed a taxi to the airport.

Flights were fully back on track after the blackout, and thankfully mine was on time. I checked in and made my way to security.

My whole body felt subdued, weighted down by the loss in my heart. It was only a few days, but in that short amount of time, Reid had opened me back up. He made me feel things I never knew I could feel, but the reality of our lives stared straight at me in the form of a nearly four-hour flight, putting two thousand miles between us.

Miles that would always be between us, making it so our fledgling relationship could never take flight.

I slipped my shoes back on, grabbed my bags, and headed down the corridor.

"Sir! Excuse me, sir, come back here!" I heard a security agent yell out.

There were a lot of mumbles, and I could swear I heard Reid's name, but I kept on the path to my gate.

"Harper!"

I turned to find Reid running toward me, shoes missing from his feet.

"Reid?" My heart thumped wildly in my chest. It wasn't an illusion, a hope. He was there, TSA hot on his heels.

He was breathing hard when he stopped in front of me. "Tell me. If I wasn't famous, would you want me?"

I shook my head. "That's beside the point."

"Answer the question."

"Yes," I whispered.

His lips crashed to mine, and the light that had slowly died over the last few days was as bright as the sun. "I'm not giving up on you, Harper."

"What?" I asked, still stunned.

"We can make this work."

"How?" My heart thumped wildly, taking over my negative thoughts and clinging to the dream.

"Let me worry about that. All you have to say is that you want me, too."

"I want you." There was never any doubt there.

He beamed at me. "I'll contact you. Every day. I know we can work."

"Sir! You need to come back to security, right now," one of the agents said, but Reid ignored them. I heard them murmuring and talking. "Is that Reid Gallagher?"

"Why so much for me?" I asked.

He brushed a few loose strands from my face. "Because."

"Because, what?"

"You're special, Harper. Once upon a time, I got some advice from a producer that if I ever got this feeling, to chase it. Weston Lockwood chased it, and it gave him the love of his life. I can't let this go until I know."

My heart slammed against my chest. "Until you know what?"

"If you're the one." He cradled my head in his hands. "For some reason, I feel it in my gut, and it's not constipation."

My bottom lip trembled. "Why do you make me feel like this?"

"Like what?"

A tear slipped down my cheek. "Like everything I ever felt before was a lie. Like the only truth is you."

He pulled me closer, his forehead resting against mine. "It's the same for me." He pressed his mouth to mine, lips parting for his tongue to meet mine. "Have a safe flight, beautiful. Let me know when you get in."

He began to step away, but I grabbed onto him and pulled him back, crashing my lips to his. "Have a good day of filming." One last soft kiss, then we reluctantly stepped back.

His smile was blinding as he backed up, and he gave me one last wink before turning toward the agents and holding his hands up. A few seconds later, agents were shaking his hand and getting selfies before leading him back to the security checkpoint.

I bit my lip, a huge smile on my face as I watched him walk away. Just as I was about to continue to my gate, he turned and cupped his hands around his mouth.

"Comets suck!"

I let out a laugh before yelling back. "And they rock your world!"

He grinned from ear to ear and nodded in agreement before disappearing from sight.

As I sat at the gate, warmth spread through me as my phone went off. It was a photo text from Reid looking all pouty.

Miss you already – Reid

EPILOGUE

"Hi," Reid said.

"What are you wearing?" I asked.

Almost a month had passed since I last saw Reid in Vegas. It still seemed like a dream and I would have brushed it off, but he stayed true to his word and contacted me every day in some form. Sometimes it was just a "Morning, beautiful" text, other times it was a three-hour-long phone conversation or an email. There were pictures and video clips almost streaming in. A dozen stars had said hi to me on video chats. He even sent me three dozen red roses for Valentine's the week before.

He chuckled. "Isn't that my line?"

"Sexist much? I want to objectify you. I mean, I am dating one of Hollywood's hottest." Though I wasn't sure dating was the right word since we never got an official date. But one night on video another actor asked, "Is that your girl?" and he replied, "Yep, my girlfriend, Harper."

"Objectify away, baby. I'll reciprocate when I see you."

"And when's that?" To be honest, the space had become grating. All I wanted, wished for, was even something as simple as the run-by kisses like we had at the hotel. Instead, I'd had to settle for a lonely bed and occasional phone sex.

Days off, like the one I was having, reminded me just how much he wasn't in my daily life. Always so far away.

"Open your front door and find out."

I froze, then craned my head toward the door, but there was no shadow in the obscure glass.

"Ha, ha, very funny."

"You're not going to check?" he asked.

"You were in Rome last night," I reminded him. There simply was no way he was at my door.

"Are you sure?"

"Is that code for you lied to me?"

"There are great advantages to chartering luxury planes."

I froze and stared at the door. If he was playing with me, I was going to smack his beautiful face the next time I saw him. I blew out a breath before flipping the deadbolt and pulling the door open.

My teeth mashed together as I stared out at nothing.

"You're an ass," I said as tears filled my eyes.

"There's a car in your driveway, baby," he said, knowing that calling me baby was enough to melt my agitation.

I walked around the front to find that there was a car, but Reid wasn't in it. However, a man in a black suit stood at the hood.

"Miss Evans."

I blinked at the man. "What's going on?"

"Go back inside and pack a bag for the weekend. Think tropical. Then get in the car. He'll bring you to the airport we're about to land at."

"Reid."

"You told me last night you didn't have work today and had no plans for the weekend."

I didn't, but it was so sudden that I was racking my brain trying to remember if there was something. "A full weekend?"

"Yeah."

The excitement of seeing him again flooded in. "Really?"

"They don't need me on set for a week. I couldn't pass it up. Now, you have twenty minutes to get packed and get that sexy ass in the car."

It was real. I was going to see him again. After so long, I wasn't sure it would ever happen, and was afraid our days in Vegas was all I would ever get.

With time being limited, I hung up the phone and ran to the bedroom to pull my suitcase down. I dug through my closet for bathing suits, shorts, tanks, tees, flip-flops; all the warm weather gear I would need. I was still in my pajamas when he called, and I threw them off and slid on the outfit I wore the day we met.

A quick mental checklist of everything I might need, then I was throwing on my coat, locking up the house, and climbing into the back of the black sedan.

As we drove, my leg bounced. I couldn't believe I was up and going on a trip. It was so spontaneous that I almost forgot to text Sarah and let her know. I wasn't sure where we were going, but after a few minutes the car turned toward a small airstrip.

Six months ago I was buried in the wreckage Jeremy left, but after meeting Reid, I realized there were feelings deeper and stronger than I ever felt with him.

Jeremy didn't destroy my life, he set it free.

We drove down the open airstrip toward a hangar. I couldn't keep the smile from my face as I looked at the waiting plane and the man leaning against the stairway. As soon as the car stopped, I jumped out and ran across the asphalt before leaping into his arms.

"Hi," I said when I pulled back.

"Hi." He let out a nervous laugh, one that overtook me, and he pulled me back to his arms. "I missed you so much."

I nuzzled into his large chest and let the warmth from his embrace soak into my skin. It was healing, and perfect on levels I couldn't comprehend. All I knew was that it was right, and being away from him was wrong.

What we had was special. We both knew it. The feeling in my heart wasn't false. Over weeks, we'd gotten to know each other on a deeper level.

He took my hand and we climbed up to the plane, my luggage taken care of by the driver. We were barely inside when I pulled him back down for a kiss.

"I don't want to be away from you for that long ever again," I said, a quiver in my voice. All my false bravado and strength washed away the second his arms were around me.

He stared down at me, his gaze bouncing between my eyes. "Move in with me."

"What?"

"Move to L.A. Live with me. Travel with me. Become a physical therapist for actors."

I blinked at him, at what he was asking. It wasn't an off-the-cuff comment. He was serious. All rational thoughts that should have been there were silenced by my heart.

None of it mattered. There was no need for him to convince me. I wanted to be wherever he was.

"Yes."

From the moment I slammed into him, I was becoming his.

It didn't matter what the future held, as long as he was beside me.

THANK YOU...

Thank you for supporting the Blackout Anthology. We sincerely hope you enjoyed each and every word! You're the reason we keep writing...

Thank you also to our host,
Private Party Book Club:

www.privatepartybookclub.com

Stay in the know:
www.privatepartybookclub.com.newsletter

About the Author

K.I. Lynn is the USA Today Bestselling Author from The Bend Anthology and the Amazon Bestsellers, Breach and Becoming Mrs Lockwood. She spent her life in the arts, everything from music to painting and ceramics, then to writing. Characters have always run around in her head, acting out their stories, but it wasn't until later in life she would put them to pen. It would turn out to be the one thing she was really passionate about.

Since she began posting stories online, she's garnered acclaim for her diverse stories and hard hitting writing style. Two stories and characters are never the same, her brain moving through different ideas faster than she can write them down as it also plots its quest for world domination...or cheese. Whichever is easier to obtain... Usually it's cheese.

Website - http://www.kilynnauthor.com/
Facebook - http://bit.ly/1qbp5tx
Twitter - https://twitter.com/KI_Lynn_
Instagram - https://www.instagram.com/k.i.lynn
Get my Newsletter - http://bit.ly/1U9NSoC

Made in the USA
Columbia, SC
15 June 2025

59415142R00081